Saving Jazz

for Nick

KATE
MᶜCAFFREY

Saving Jazz

 FREMANTLE PRESS

Prologue

It's the silence that's disturbing. Silence that has spanned the last few days. Long silence, accompanied by moody staring out of the window or into the distance. Silence that allows nothing to be said, and nothing to be heard. Silence that speaks volumes.

Something is up. I know this, but nothing I say elicits a response. No amount of specific questions, or even diversionary questions, break through the impenetrable wall of silence. She won't speak to me. And I can't read her face, impassive; her body language, protective; her silence, deafening.

It is killing me.

It's been over half an hour since we got home. She said nothing on the journey. Even before it, when I insisted she stay at school until the end of the day, she *met me with silence. She switched her phone off. What could I do, but pick her up early for the second day in a row and hope she would speak.*

But she was silent. And now she still is.

Forty minutes.

That's enough. I get out of my floral armchair, place my cup on the table and walk upstairs. I bang on her bathroom door.

Nothing.

Silence.

'Annie,' I call out loudly, trying to harness my rising hysteria. 'Open the door. I want to talk.'

Nothing.

I grab the brass handle. I turn it. The door silently refuses me entry.

'Annie, open this door.'

I want to scream. Bang the door down because the silence is crashing down on top of me. 'Annie,' I shout again and rattle the handle furiously.

Silence.

I pull the drawers from the antique hall stand. One cracks as it hits the floor, spewing contents out. I rummage through them. A hairpin. I stick it in the door's release mechanism. I rattle the handle furiously again, loudly, because what other option is there?

The handle gives and the door pushes open so hard I hear the wall chip behind it. 'Annie,' I scream as the word freezes on my lips. 'Annie,' I try to say again, running to my child, my beautiful daughter, Annie of acting classes and impersonations, Annie who wanted to be a unicorn as a five-year-old and travel the world as a fifteen-year-old, but there are no words. The silence has infected me.

I run to the bathtub. Her hair swirls across the water like an oil spill. I plunge my arms through the water, grabbing at her shoulders. She slips through my fingers. Water sloshes over my feet. I clutch at her shoulders again. I try not to look at her face. A bluish hue. Her eyes are shut. In my head I'm saying 'Annie, Annie' as she falls onto me, so wet, so heavy. I wrestle with her lifeless body on the floor and I'm still speaking to her. I begin CPR. I can't remember how many breaths to how many pumps. I just keep doing it and pull my mobile out of my pocket.

I hear someone's voice in the silence. 'I need an ambulance,' it says clearly and calmly. I breathe — three inhales, fifteen pumps.

'My daughter's not breathing,' the voice continues.

'Yes, I'm administering CPR.' The voice gives the address of my house. I continue breathing for her, beating her heart. I can't stop. I hear the sirens. Footsteps and voices break the silence. Hands gently remove me and they are there making her breathe, making her heart beat.

'Are you the one who called triple-0?' one of the paramedics asks me.

I can't take my eyes off my daughter. 'Yes,' I say, in that same calm and clear voice that broke the silence.

WHAT IT'S LIKE
TO BE A GIRL

Welcome to my blog. This is a blog of confessions about Greenheadgate and the reality of what it's actually, really, truly like to be a girl ...

DISCLAIMER: *To protect the privacy of others, names have been changed and characters combined. While I have attempted to be as honest and truthful as I can, these are my memories; I am the teller of my own story.*

'It is far harder to kill a phantom than a reality.'
Virginia Woolf
The Death of the Moth and Other Essays

Post 1: In the beginning

My name is Jasmine Lovely, Jazz usually (unless I'm in trouble), and I'm a rapist. In fact, I'm guilty of more than just rape but, as my lawyer says, in the interests of judicial fairness, we can't be prejudicial. It's hard enough to admit to rape. As a girl, it's exceptionally hard. People look at you blankly. Not that it's something I admit to often, like I just did to you. I don't normally preface my introductions with that abrupt statement, and I'm not part of a self-help group, where you hold your hand up, state your name, then your addiction, affliction, crime. But this is the truth. I'm sixteen now, but twelve months ago that is what I did, I raped a girl. Her name was Annie Townshend. I could sound all David Copperfield and say, 'To begin my life with the beginning of my life, I record that I was born (as I have been informed and believe) on a Friday,' but I'm not recording this for posterity. In fact, I'm really just creating this blog to address everything, to set the record straight.

For those of you choosing to follow my blog (and, I might add, you probably need to get a life if the ramblings of a sixteen-year-old constitute your week's entertainment), I should go back further, before the night that changed everything. As the power of the internet allows anyone around the globe to have access to this site I guess I need (as Miss Peters, my Lit teacher, says) to give you some context.

I lived in a small town called Greenhead about a hundred kilometres out of Perth. It's a pretty quiet place, mostly small farm holdings, big houses and the local primary school. It's a place where wildflowers grow in abundance and one of the big trades is exporting them to the rest of the world. If you've ever had a delivery of Geraldton wax or kangaroo paws, they probably came from Greenhead. The other big trade is wine. Over the last twenty years plenty of boutique wineries have popped up. It's made the landscape more attractive — big stone tasting cellars and an influx of tourists — which makes the place more vibrant, particularly in the summer. The knock-on effect was the creation of a town centre, a bakery, cafe, newsagent and convenience store. It sounds smaller than it is — I feel like I'm giving the wrong impression. It's not *that* country, by country standards. The people who live there are mostly well heeled. Enough disposable income to take yearly holidays, drive nice cars, have quad bikes. Most of the kids yearn for the day they can leave — get closer to the action, or at least closer to a train station, which is about an hour away. So I guess the geography made us kind of insular — we had to find stuff to do within walking distance, because until we got our own cars, we were pretty well stuck. There were about thirty of us who travelled each day, by bus, to Namba High, the closest high school, nearly forty minutes away. It's not large, by city standards — maybe four hundred from Year 7 to Year 12 — so everyone knows everyone, although the degrees of friendship vary. To the rest of the school we were the Greenhead kids. Sometimes I think they viewed us as a bit country, and now I wonder if that attitude is what fuelled us to party harder than them.

We had a reputation for big nights at friends' places when their parents were out of town. That was the upside to the isolation: if your parents had to go to Perth, they normally stayed the night, and we seized every opportunity to capitalise on their absence. We had gatherings about once a month. The gatherings were always the same — steal booze from your parents and take it to the party. The one goal was to get as trashed as possible, as early as possible. When Scottie McGough discovered jagerbombs, things got even messier. Wasted by nine, passed out wherever you fell, hung-over for a couple of days. It was just what we did. But again, I feel like I'm jumping ahead too fast and maybe giving you the wrong impression. Aside from the parties, the only other big thing we had was school. So we would travel as a group, see each other in classes and travel home. Most of us worked for our parents in some capacity and did schoolwork. It was a pretty sedate life — until a gathering was scheduled and then there was something to really look forward to. But I guess it's school that tipped the balance we

Greenheads had. School and the internet — Facebook in particular, but also Snapchat and Instagram. I think without those things that connected us to the Namba kids, and to the rest of the world, everything might not have got so bad.

I guess you want to know who the main players were. Me, of course, Jazz Lovely. What can I tell you about myself? You should know me, before you judge me. I think this is one of my main reasons for exposing everything about the night we call Greenheadgate. I'm being judged based on my actions of one night. It's like everything I did before that evening has ceased to exist and the sum total of who I am is encapsulated in the word 'rapist'. I admit it's true — and while I may not have stated this earlier, I am deeply and profoundly ashamed of my actions. The worst thing about regret is that there is no way to undo it. No way to go back in time and make better choices. No way to prevent the here and now. Please don't think I want you to feel sympathetic — what I did was terrible, a crime, something I can't change despite all the wishing and regret in the world. I wish it didn't have to define me, I struggle daily to live with my actions. But live with them I must — because there is no other option. Annie Townshend thought there was and I understand why. Both she and I made terrible mistakes that night. The difference is I'm prepared to live with mine.

So, about me: I'm 172 centimetres, 58 kilos and I have a really pretty face. I imagine you just rolled your eyes in disgust — totally up myself — but there is no point in lying on this blog. No point in false modesty — that was a big contributing factor to the events, along with jealousy and self-esteem issues. I know I'm pretty, I've always been noticed by boys, even some men. I have a classical face and huge blue eyes. My eyelashes drive my girlfriends mad, they are so long and fake looking, but they're real. I've even been approached in the city by strangers asking if I'd like to be a model — and that is what I thought I'd do, up until the night of Greenheadgate. But now I want to finish school, I want a degree. Who knows now if that is possible? But anyway, here is the thing about being pretty. You don't have to try very hard. You get offered opportunities, people want to get to know you. So, what I'm about to say contradicts this (please don't think me a liar — I'm not. I'd just like to make that clear, throughout all of this I never told one lie): because you don't have to work hard to attract people and opportunities, you have to work harder than most to keep them. On one level people are drawn to beautiful faces and at the same time they hate them.

I have to be smart at school, because if I'm not, there is always someone there ready to claim, 'She might be pretty, but she's as thick as pig shit.' I have to work hard to be fit or it's, 'She might have a beautiful face but it's a shame about her body.' And more than anything I have to have a nice, friendly personality or it's, 'Yeah, she's lovely in name and lovely to look at but what a fucking bitch.' I worked hard, I tried really hard — and I hope this doesn't sound like I'm a phony, but that is genuinely who I am. Was. I tried not to have faults, because, as Jack once told me, this world is a bitch and people even bitchier. But of course all the trying in the world can't make you perfect. What is perfection? I had the same doubts and fears as my friends, the same appearance issues if there was a pimple lurking, the same body issues — because despite my seeming perfection I am flat chested. Boobs not even big enough to fill a B cup.

That might seem like the most meaningless thing you've ever heard, but there it is, my Achilles heel. Mark Ward in my year had bigger tits than me. Make no mistake, he was punished mercilessly for that crime against humanity. But that was my focus — the size of my boobs — and for a long time I really thought that if they were bigger (I certainly wouldn't have ruled out plastic surgery) then I could cope with anything. Before you think it, let me say it: how fucking shallow was that? But we were shallow, all of us, fixating on minor flaws and using them to make ourselves miserable, or using them as a weapon against someone else.

But body issues aside, before the night of Greenheadgate I was a mostly happy and content person. I had friends, I was popular and I was doing well at school. I had no real dramas in my life. And even my mum and dad, who worked together in our boutique winery, were proud of me, in their aloof kind of way. It kills me now, to know how much that has changed.

Post 2: Best friends for life

I guess you want to know about my friends. Let me take you further back in time to when I was six. It was time to live the dream: after arriving from South Africa as a newlywed couple, my parents' idea was always to make money, then leave the city and buy a small landholding where they could grow things and live in a safe community. My dad retired from his lucrative dental practice and bought fifty acres in Greenhead to set up a winery. My mum, who was a bank manager, had been studying viticulture. I was starting Grade 1 and it was the biggest upheaval of my life. As we stood in front of the school in Greenhead I was terrified of being left alone, but along came this six-year-old boy, Jack West, and his mum, Maria.

'Hey,' Jack said, scrunching up his eyes, as he still does today when he smiles, 'what grade are you in?'

'One,' I said, looking at his tousled red hair and freckly face.

'Me too. I'm Jack.' He waved to his mum. 'See ya. Come on,' he grabbed my hand, 'let's make sure we get to sit together.'

Jack always took me by the hand, from that day on. He was my best friend in the whole world. I trusted him with everything. One day I was at his house while my mum was at the hairdresser. After exhausting all of the Disney DVDs, Jack had an idea — he would be my hairdresser. I sat patiently on the blue plastic stool as Jack tied a towel around my neck and arranged his tools.

'Right,' he said, 'and how would you like your hair today?'

I waved him on. 'However,' I said. My hair was shoulder-length ringlets — my mother's pride and joy — held aloft, either side of my face, in two bunches.

'Something fashionable,' Jack said in his best imitation of a hairdresser.

It was Maria's scream, when she entered the

playroom carrying two glasses of Milo and a plate of biscuits (that Milo stain never left the cream carpet), that alerted me to the fact that Jack's cut was definitely *not* fashionable.

'Good lord, what have you done?' Maria shrieked, collecting my perfect bunch, still in its elastic band, off the floor. Jack had severed it from my head, just above my ear.

When my mother arrived, her newly coiffured hair unable to even bob under its helmet of hairspray, her look of disappointment (one she perfected later, during the time of Greenheadgate) confirmed she agreed with Maria.

She stared grimly through the windscreen as she drove me to the local salon. My mum always worried about what the neighbours would think. She couldn't see anything funny in this.

'Cut it above her ear,' she ordered the startled hairdresser, holding my remaining bunch out as an offering.

'Such beautiful ringlets,' the girl murmured. 'Why?'

'Here's why,' Mum said, turning my head so the girl could see my asymmetrical cut. 'Even it up.'

When the girl offered my mother the lopped-off bunch as a keepsake, my mother, no fan of sentimentality, dismissed it with a wave of her hand. 'Bin it,' she said. I know that even today, Maria still has the other one in a box of Jack's childhood memories.

So from the age of six I sported a very chic bob, which I actually loved. However, after my twelfth birthday, my dad (back in the days when he actually looked me in the eye) commented scathingly, 'What do you think you are? Parisian? For crying out loud, Jasmine, grow it — no girl needs to look like a boy, or French for that matter.' From then on, I let my hair grow out.

As for me and Jack, we didn't care, it was just hair. We were six. We were best friends for life.

Post 3: He's just a boy

All through primary school it was Jack and me.

One hot summer day, when we were about ten, Jack and I were mucking around with a pot of bubble liquid and a bubble blower. You know those plastic rings on a stick that you dip into the detergent and blow through? We had been to Scottie's party and got them in a lolly bag. We were seeing who could blow the biggest one — Jack was dragging his plastic ring through the air, creating a distorted and bulging bubble that reflected streaks of blue and pink in the sunlight. Suddenly the bubble broke free from its plastic confines and wobbled through the air, over the hedge that separated Jack's place from the Maitlands'.

We pushed through the hedge and watched

the bubble shiver through the air and slowly settle on the surface of the Maitlands' pond. Despite the trickling water from the ornamental stone fish's mouth, which rippled the water, the bubble sat firmly on top of the pond. It was indestructible. That was until a large pair of lips, belonging to one of Mr Maitland's gigantic koi, puckered up and kissed its side. The bubble popped. The expression on the koi's face was one of sheer shock (I think startled looks are the default position in these creatures anyway), but no matter, it had us in fits of laughter. And then a thought bubble popped right over the top of Jack's head.

'I've got a great idea,' he said.

We gathered up detergent from both our houses and squirted it — all of it — into the stone fish's mouth where it spewed water into the pond. It was immediate. The pond started foaming violently and then it went out of control. Our laughter stopped abruptly as a tsunami of foam cascaded over the confines of the pond and erupted down Greenhead's main road.

'The fish,' Jack shouted as we watched one helpless victim caught up in the deluge skitter down the street. I ran to my house to grab a bucket and something to scoop. In the time it took me to find a ladle — the one with the holes in it — and return to Jack, it was too late.

'Geez, Jazz,' Jack said, really ashamed and miserable. 'I didn't think that through. I think I killed all the fish.'

We hadn't. There was one left, who we rescued from the dishwater and popped in the bucket with clean water. Jack was so brave marching into Mr Maitland's bakery and confessing to the crime, while I stood behind him holding the bucket with the sole survivor. I'll never forget Mr Maitland's face — the dark beetroot colour it went, the spittle flying from his lips as he berated Jack and labelled him (for life) the town troublemaker.

Others in the town found it funny. Not the death of the fish, which Jack solemnly promised to replace — they just knew Jack was trying to have a laugh and was not intentionally malicious. 'He's just a boy,' was the usual response.

Post 4: Here's Tommy

Tommy Robinson arrived at Namba High at the start of Year 8. He was totally hot — all the girls had instant crushes on him. A perfect face, with perfect teeth. I wasn't alone in fantasising that one day Tommy would be my boyfriend. The guys liked him too. He was athletic — into footy, so a welcome addition to the local team. Tommy slid easily into the Namba community.

But I guess I had doubts about him pretty early on. He'd watch me and Jack together and make comments.

'What's up between you two?' Tommy asked once as we were all sitting around at school.

'Nothing,' Jack said dismissively.

'You fancy her.' It was a statement, not a question.

I turned on him, ready to set him straight as to how Jack was my best friend and that was it. But Jack replied first.

'Aww, gross,' he said, screwing up his face. 'As if I fancy her. That's Jazz.'

I was humiliated and hurt. I got up and walked off. I didn't speak to Jack for the rest of the day. How dare he say that, like that? How dare he?

The next morning I was still studiously avoiding him. He found me outside Food Tech.

'Hey,' he said, like nothing had happened, 'when King tells us to get the ingredients, you get extra chocolate — I think the muffins will need more than the one piece they'll let us have.' He screwed his eyes up, laughing, but stopped when he saw I wasn't joining in. 'What's up?'

'Nothing,' I said, turning away. I didn't want to talk to him, I didn't want to be around him and I certainly didn't want to be doing his dirty work.

'Sure,' he said frowning.

'I'm not your little bitch,' I snapped.

'Hey, steady, what's your problem?' Jack said.

'Get stuffed, Jack.' I really wanted to tell him to *fuck off*, but then, when I was thirteen, I think it was like the worst thing I could think of saying. To actually say it to Jack, my Jack, was impossible.

'Hey,' he grabbed my arm, 'what?'

'How can you touch me,' I shook him off, 'when I'm so gross?' And I couldn't help the tears, so I ran to the toilets.

Jack pushed open the door to the girls' toilets and saw me sobbing over the sink. 'You'll be in serious trouble if Mr Man finds you in here,' I snivelled at him through the mirror. Mr Man was the actual name of our deputy, a man mountain whose appearance belied his generally soft interior. Still, he wasn't one who would take lightly a boy breaching the sanctity of the girls' toilets. I could already hear him: 'Show respect — they are young women, who are entitled to privacy.'

'I don't care,' Jack said, venturing forwards. 'Jazzy, I'd cut my tongue from my head if I thought I'd offended you.'

'Well, I wish I had a knife,' I said, glaring at him angrily, 'because you have.'

'I didn't mean it like that,' Jack said. 'I didn't mean *you* were gross. I meant what he was suggesting was gross. You're my best friend. You're like my sister. You're more than that, you're my everything in the whole world. The idea that it's something else is gross. Guys like Tommy don't understand.'

As usual, Jack had pulled the anger from me. Of course he hadn't meant it like that. Of course he was repulsed that someone would think he had an ulterior motive towards me. Jack loved me. Best friends for life.

'But no matter what, I'm sorry, Jazzy.' And he put his arms around me and hugged me tightly.

Later that week, I got my first period. I sat on my bed sobbing, because — well, I didn't know why, but I just felt so sad and confused. And Jack sat with me. He held my hand. He went to the shop and bought me two different types of pads, because he wasn't sure if wings were good or not. He never blamed my changing body and my hormones for making me so prickly. He never treated me like I was a mere female who couldn't control her emotions. He just held my hand.

And as for Tommy, well, from that day I never

trusted him. I guess I always felt like he was looking for something nasty in everything that was innocent.

Of course I also had girlfriends, picked up over the years at Greenhead. Simone, Sim we called her, whose dad was a cop — so you can bet there were never any gatherings at her place — and also Lily, whose parents had a huge wildflower business. We were all the same age so it made sense that we would hang together. And, in the middle of Year 9, along came Annie (you'll get to know her later).

So that's the backdrop against which this tragic tale is set — a small community, and the fact that bad decisions can have life-changing effects.

Post 5: *The bad app*

It was twelve months ago, although it seems like more than a year. Summer had truly hit with nuclear force and the air was full of the drone of bees in the grevilleas. The sun was hot by 7 am and the holidays were already a lifetime ago. School had just started and we were already waiting for the first term break.

The second week of Year 10 — nothing to report, classes pretty much the same, most teachers unchanged. There was a sense of relief to know the Head of Maths had finally retired — it surprised us that she was able to face sunlight when she dragged herself from her fur-lined coffin each morning. Finally someone had pushed a stake through the old vampire's heart (not that I'm admitting to *that* crime). We partied in Maths that day, and Miss

Cormoron — more terrified of the Head of Maths than we were — celebrated the most. But aside from the usual beginnings, there was nothing unusual about the beginning.

'Did you see this?' Jack pushed his phone across the canteen table to me. I was so hot I'd taken my school shoes off, but I was paranoid my feet stank. So I was focusing more on any potential odours than whatever had been occupying Jack and Tommy for most of the break.

'Who is it?' I asked looking at a pair of ample breasts on the screen.

'Scroll across, there's more,' Jack said.

There were seven images. Big round boobs, then shots of the boobs and the top of a flimsy black g-string. The next picture showed the bottom of her face. She'd been careful to keep her identity secret, but only one person at Namba High had a beauty spot like that above their lip.

'Casey?' I asked surprised. I never thought in a million years she would take nude selfies — and why was she sending them to Jack?

'Yeah,' he took the phone from me and handed it

to Tommy. 'They're not mine, they're his.'

'Why?' I asked Tommy. Don't get me wrong, I'm not a total prude, but you'd have to be a moron to send nude selfies and expect them to stay private. Back in Year 8 there was a massive scandal with a group of Namba girls and the whole sexting thing. It was standard stuff — a guy you liked would text, 'Send me a picture and I'll send one back.' So girls did. They took pictures of themselves totally nude and sent it to their crush — sometimes they'd get one back, but most often not. Then he'd share it with his friends and before too long most people at school had seen them. It was huge. The girls would then get slut-shamed, while the boys were free of any judgement. For the boys it was like their rite of passage, but if a chick did it, she was a whore. The scandal broke when someone's phone was found at school and one of the deputies, Mr Deaks, accessed the images. The offender was called in, the net was cast and most of the male Year 8 cohort dragged in for questioning. After that, the school ran these stupid seminars on The Dangers of Sexting, thinking it was going to change anyone's behaviour. Maybe a few people thought about it, particularly when we were educated on the whole 'being in possession of and distributing child porn' stuff. But no one really bought that bullshit anyway. How can one thirteen-year-old sending a picture of herself to her boyfriend be distributing kiddie porn? Anyway, after that things became covert — particularly with the benefit of Snapchat. It was safe sexting.

'A new game,' Tommy said, not lifting his eyes from the screen. 'It's called Tits or Tops. Guess which option Casey took?'

'That is so stupid.' I felt really pissed off with her. Not because her boobs were fantastic — and even girls with tits bigger than mine would feel something akin to jealousy — but to play this game, for the satisfaction of these boys? Did she have no self-respect?

'She doesn't know I've got them,' Tommy leaned closer. 'We were playing it on Snapchat.'

'Then how do you have them?' I asked.

'Got this app. A guy I was playing *GTA* with told me about it. It lets you capture the images without the sender knowing. So Casey might think she flashed her tits for five seconds — but in reality I can look at them as often as I like. And share them with my mates,' Tommy said.

I could feel my lip curl. What a total pig. 'It's wrong,' I said.

'If Casey wants to put on a show, why wouldn't we watch?' Jack said. I frowned at him. I hated the way Jack was around Tommy, stupid big-man talk about girls. This wasn't the Jack I'd grown up with, who'd always protected me. This was someone else, someone I really didn't like.

'I think it's unfair if you shift the rules without saying,' I said, pulling my shoes on.

'Shit Jazz, don't be so uptight,' Tommy said. 'It's not like anyone will ask to see your little titties.'

'Go fuck yourself, Tommy,' I said getting up and stalking off.

I was furious. With Tommy, of course, but also Jack. The whole way they viewed girls made it hard for us. Tommy's snide remark about my boobs was an example. They ridiculed us for the way we looked, and then wanted us to show them our body parts. In Art I watched Casey. I wondered if she knew, if she had been told about the photos. I knew it wouldn't take long for her to find out. I felt so bad for her.

It was all over Facebook that night. I sat in my

room and watched the hate on my mobile.

Ho alert. If you think this girl is a whore then click Like.

It had 235 Likes. And then there were comments. The gender divide was huge — most of the guys made mention of what a great rack she had, how they'd like a piece of that and other general 'thanks' or 'made my night' comments. But the girls! The vitriol, the hatred: whore, slut, ho — not one girl sympathised, or criticised the male comments. No one defended Casey — and she didn't even try to defend herself. Not one girl stood up for her, even though plenty of them had done the same. The big thing was, if you hadn't been caught then you were clean. So much judgement.

The next day at school Casey was absent, but I saw plenty of people huddled around phones. And even though it wasn't me in the images, it was hard not to feel paranoid for her. I just knew this wasn't going to go away in a hurry.

'She deserves it,' Sim said to me in Maths. 'She took the pictures — no one made her.'

'But haven't you done it too?' I asked.

'Yeah, but I took the Top option,' Sim said, 'I'm not a whore.'

That was the atmosphere building up to the gathering.

Post 6: Get a life

.

It was like everyone was waiting for Casey's return.
Would she show her face the next day? Would she
continue to hide, having been slut-shamed? I guess I
was as surprised as anyone when I saw her walking
down the halls at school the following day. I watched
her, tall and proud, defiant in each stride as she
purposefully made her way to her home room. If she
noticed the guys still huddling around phones and
smirking at her, she seemed to ignore it. I have to
admit I was even more surprised by this response. I
think I expected her to shrivel and die of shame, but
she didn't, and her girlfriends — no matter what they
secretly thought — stood firm beside her.

It erupted in the canteen area. Casey was
seated at the metal tables with two of her friends,

eating lunch. Leanne, one of the most popular girls, approached. Leanne had rolled her skirt up (the way most of us did), way up (more so than most of us), and leant across the table.

'Nice photo,' Leanne sneered. Casey didn't even look up. She continued to eat her salad roll and talk to Katie. 'Although perhaps next time you might want to keep your bra on.' I think Leanne was about to leave but Casey looked up and levelled her with a defiant stare.

'Why?' she asked, and I have to admit it sounded like a genuine query.

'Because ...' Leanne faltered and looked to her friends for support. They all gave her those same looks of disgust I'd seen on the faces of most of the other girls. 'Because you look like a whore.'

'Do I?' Casey said. 'And how many whores have you ever seen, aside from your own reflection?' Leanne opened her mouth to speak but Casey pressed on. 'Your boyfriend didn't seem to think I looked like one when he commented on my photo last night. I would think he'd be more interested in *your* actions than my appearance.'

Leanne went bright red and leant across the

bench. 'Don't you fucking mess with me,' she hissed. 'I'll smash your teeth in.'

Casey stood up. Leanne took a step back. 'Don't you mess with *me*,' Casey warned, really coldly. 'We all know about your little holiday hook-up with Sean, behind Ian's back. We all saw *those* photos. So why don't you shut your hypocritical mouth and get a life.'

If it had been a scene from a Hollywood teen film all the kids would have stood and cheered Casey. She was so brave to stand up to Leanne. So brave to defend herself.

'You're a filthy ho,' Leanne snapped, ready to walk (no doubt scared of injury to her own $7,500 orthodontic smile). But Casey wasn't ready to let it go.

'And the next time you think it's funny to dare the Year 7 girls to flash their tits on Snapchat, just remember you don't know how many people captured those photos of you with Sean.'

'Fuck off,' Leanne snarled, indicating to her friends to leave.

That night on Facebook Casey went even further.

She posted a selfie showing her entire face, her arm covering her nipples, her taut abdomen and the very hint of the top of her g-string, with the words:

I'll do what I like with my body

She received 328 Likes — and nearly all the comments were complimentary, if not totally sleazy. And despite some of the girls constantly trying to remind her that she was a slut, it seemed Casey had ended the attacks against her. It was weird — the girls continued to harass her on Facebook but the guys had moved on. Her images had been replaced by whatever was happening in the footy or rugby, or what was going down on *GTA*.

Post 7: Meet Annie

It's time for you to get acquainted with Annie
Townshend.

If Greenheadgate had never occurred I think
Annie would always have remained that girl you
remember vaguely from school — at least in the
minds of the Namba kids. Annie was my best
girlfriend, though not from the beginning, like
Sim and Lily. Annie started by hanging on our
periphery. She had always been friends with Meg
and Darcy, quieter girls in Greenhead who never
attended the gatherings. But in the middle of Year 9
Annie changed. She started to wear her school skirt
shorter — rolling it up the way we, in the popular
group, did. She often had a dark bra under her white
school blouse. She began seeing James Mitchell,

a Namba boy who was in Year 11, and she started hanging out with us more.

Annie had a really pretty face, but she was short, tiny — like a doll. At about 155 centimetres, she came up to my shoulder. And she had D-cup boobs. I know it's starting to sound like this blog is tits, tits, tits — and to a large extent it is. But, like me, Annie was hugely self-conscious about the size of her boobs.

'They make me look fat,' Annie would say, 'and they're so fucking heavy.' Assessing them I'd guess they weighed a good few kilos each.

'You don't look fat,' I said as we were shopping online. It was one of the ways we got clothes in Greenhead. 'You look like you've got big boobs and a tiny waist.'

'What about these?' Annie clicked on low-slung shorts and a bright-coloured crop top. 'Maybe that's the way to go, draw all the attention to my stomach.' She lifted her top up — she had a flat and toned tummy.

'I think that'd look good,' I said. I was also purchasing similar shorts — they were in at the time and despite the anger I felt about the way boys treated us, I still subscribed to the same game: look as hot as possible.

Annie wore that outfit the night of Greenheadgate, and she did look hot.

It was Drama class that brought us together. On stage Annie transformed into a totally different person from the shy, quiet girl who hung out with the seriously smart kids. She could become any character, affect any accent, assume any identity. I was in awe of her acting abilities. And funny, my God, she used to have me in fits of laughter. The Drama teacher, Mr White, would give us improvisations to do and Annie was the only one who could take a character and a prop to hilarious levels. I found myself always wanting to team up with her — you could guarantee that with Annie you'd deliver the finest improv in class. It flowed over, into recess and lunch, and soon I just expected to walk up to our group and find Annie already there, regaling our friends with some story, or imitating one of the teachers. The girl was skilled.

I'll never forget the day we had a relief teacher for Science. He entered the room, a shortish dark-haired man with a pencil moustache. But his stand-out feature was his wonky eye. I think it might have been glass or something, but it sat like a gigantic marble in his head, rolling around every which way. Anyway, Annie and I were at the back of class. She was telling me about some fight she'd had with James when the relief teacher, Mr Kelan, said, 'You, girl at the back, stop talking.'

Annie and I looked up, but he wasn't looking at her, so she continued telling me about the saga with James. 'So,' she whispered, 'he totally freaked out when he knew I'd hooked up with Tony before that night at Casey's when I got with him ...' She paused, hearing Mr Kelan raise his voice.

'You, girl at the back, stop talking.'

We both looked up, but again, he wasn't looking at Annie.

'So,' Annie whispered, 'I say, you know what, James, we weren't together and what I did before I met you is really none of your business ...'

She was interrupted by Mr Kelan, who had now walked halfway down the room and was pointing an irate finger at us. Spittle flew from his lips as he shouted, 'YOU, GIRL AT THE BACK OF THE ROOM. STOP TALKING.'

We both looked at him. Annie pointed to her chest. 'Who? Me? Do you mean me?'

'Who the hell do you think I'm looking at?' Mr Kelan snarled.

Innocently, so, so innocently, Annie shrugged and said, 'Frankly I've got no idea who you're looking at.'

'GET OUT,' he roared.

Post 8: Girls just wanna have fun

When I think back on my friendship with Annie all I remember is laughter and fun. In fact, I have scoured my brain to remember one incident where she got pissy with me over something, took offence, acted like a bitch. But I can honestly say that up until that night of Greenheadgate we never had a cross moment between us. And it saddens me to think that if that night had never happened, she would have been my best friend forever.

I remember this one night her mum had taken us late-night shopping in Namba. Annie and I were walking around the shops, looking at the latest fashion, buying Boost juice, and generally just hanging, when her phone pinged.

'Who is it?' I asked.

'Mum,' she said, her fingers flying over the keypad, not looking up. 'She reckons we've got ten minutes.'

'Okay,' I hung up the pink top I was going to try on.

'What are you doing?' she asked.

'We've gotta go,' I said.

'We've got ten.' She pulled the top back down. 'Try it.'

As I tried the top on, Annie sat outside the change room. I heard her phone ping every couple of seconds, and the furious tapping of her fingers as she replied. I assessed the top. It was cute. But was it worth forty dollars? Eventually I decided yes, and was just putting my t-shirt back on when I heard Annie exclaim loudly, 'Shit.' I didn't even have time to respond. She whipped the curtain back.

'What?' I said alarmed.

'Shit, oh shit,' Annie collapsed on the bench and held her phone in front of her. 'What a massive cock-up.'

'What?' I said.

'Mum keeps texting me,' Annie looked at her phone screen and started reading.

MUM
**10 min outside Dymocks. I've got to
pick up Jap**

ANNIE
DW, we'll be there. Who's Jap?

MUM
What's DW?

ANNIE
**Haha, you think you're such a tech
savvy genious**

She paused and looked up. 'But I spell

genius *genious*, with an *o*. Mum comes back with,'

MUM
**For such an English genius I'd think
you'd be able to spell it right. Wot's
DW?**

ANNIE
Don't worry

She paused again and looked at me. 'At this stage
I guess I forget it is Mum I'm texting and it's all a bit
of banter, it's like I'm texting a friend, like you.'

'Right,' I said, paying for the top at the counter,
'so what have you done?'

Annie read from her phone again.

MUM
**I'm not worried. But I can't be late. I
have to pick up Jap**

Annie looked up from the screen. 'Now, it's the second time she's mentioned this person. I've got no idea who it is and so I reply,'

ANNIE
Who the fuck is Jap

Annie looked at me breathlessly.

'You sent that to your mum?'

'I know,' Annie shook her head and howled with laughter. 'I just texted that to my own mother!'

We got to the exit near Dymocks, and Annie's mum's car was parked in the drop-off zone. Annie opened the door and we slid into the back seat.

'Hi Mum,' Annie said cheerily.

'Hi girls.' Annie's mum looked over the headrest and winked at me. 'Nice message to send your mum, Annie.'

'Mum, I'm so sorry,' Annie started apologising. 'Seriously, I forgot it was you. We don't normally have conversations. We normally send like one or two texts. I didn't mean it. I'm so sorry.'

'It's okay,' her mum held her hand up, 'DW.'

Annie and I both laughed. I marvelled at her mum. My own mother would have had a nervous breakdown reading that message from me. It would have been serious and stern discussions about the appropriate use of language and technology. God knows, my phone would have been taken for at least a week by my father and I would've been grounded until I was thirty.

When we pulled up at Annie's house her mum told us to bring in the shopping, as she got the Japanese food from the front seat. Jap — of course. When we entered the house Annie's dad greeted us at the front door.

'Hi guys,' he said grabbing some of the shopping. 'Hey Annie, who the fuck's Jap?'

'Dad!' she shouted and they both laughed.

We walked into the dining room, where the table was set and the plastic containers of food opened. Maggie, Annie's ten-year-old sister, was already scooping teriyaki chicken onto her plate. 'Hey Jazz,' she said, looking up. 'Hey Annie, who the fuck is Jap?'

Behind us Annie's parents roared with laughter. 'Definitely one for the eighteenth, kiddo,' her mum said sitting down. 'I will never forget this.'

'And you'll never live it down,' her dad said.

Post 9: Are video games really harmless?

I pushed open the door to Jack's room. As usual it stank of footwear and sweaty clothes. His bed was unmade and the curtains drawn. He was in front of his computer, with a headset on, shouting at someone who was not in the room.

'Take the bitch!' Jack said. I watched over his shoulder as two guys punched a woman in the face.

'What is that?' I asked.

'A dirty whore,' Jack said and then logged off. 'Science?'

I shrugged at this Other Jack, the one that played games that abused women, the one I didn't like. I wanted to get through our Science project but it was hard to turn off, as Jack did, from images like that.

'Sure,' I pulled out my lab report and bit the end of my pen.

'What's up?' he asked after a few minutes of silence.

I shrugged. 'Nothing.'

He let another few minutes go by.

'Have I pissed you off?' he asked.

I shrugged again.

'What have I done?' he asked.

'I don't know, Jack,' I said sarcastically, 'playing that stupid game, the stupid things that come out of your mouth. Acting like a dick.' I was surprised by the words, by the anger I felt for him.

'Steady on,' Jack held up his hand. 'It's not real, Jazz. They're cartoon characters, if you hadn't noticed.'

I was starting to feel over the top, like I was being a bit hysterical.

'Jazz, it's just a stupid game,' Jack said, annoyed with me.

'It's not just the game, Jack,' I said angrily, 'it's the way you boys treat us. I'm not sure if it's because we live in this small fucking place, or if it's because Greenhead is the Misogynists' Capital of Australia.'

'That's a bit harsh,' Jack said. 'How are we all suddenly women-haters because of a few computer graphics?'

'It leaches out,' I said, 'into the real world. Into sexualising girls like they're just things, objects. Into the way you speak and act. The way you view women.'

'Man, you sound like an angry lesbian,' Jack snapped.

'And you sound like a potential rapist,' I fired back.

'Oh, I see,' Jack said angrily. 'You're suggesting that all guys who play *GTA* are going to go on to be rapists. That's a bit of a stretch. It's like saying people who play *COD* are going to go and gun down strangers. The evidence isn't there.'

'Isn't it, though?' I said, frowning, the anger dissipating with his argument. 'We watched *Bowling for Columbine*, and Dylan and Eric did watch violent games and did go out and gun people down.'

'It's a fallacious argument,' Jack said, far more calmly. 'There are plenty of people who play those games and don't act it out. You know that.'

'I don't buy it,' I said. 'How is it possible that

those games don't desensitise you? Don't shape your attitudes towards women and sex and violence?'

'They just don't,' Jack said flatly. 'We recognise that it's just a game. That's all.'

I shook my head. Sure, I agreed with some of what he was saying – if everyone who played those games committed crimes then we would live in a war zone. But it had to have an impact, right?

'Maybe not everyone then,' I said, 'but it must affect some warped and twisted people.'

'Like?' Jack asked.

'Tommy.' It was the first name that popped into my head.

'Dude, what is the matter with you? We know Tommy. He's not like that.'

'Those photos,' I said.

Jack got up and pushed his chair away. 'Seriously, Jazz, that's a totally different thing. Tommy didn't take them against Casey's will. She took them of herself. She sent them on Snapchat.'

'But he saved them and shared them,' I was starting to feel confused.

'She gave her permission.'

'She so did not!' Now I jumped up from my chair

and stood angrily opposite him, my arms folded tightly across my chest. I hate to admit it but I was feeling like this was unwinnable.

'We're not in Grade 5 anymore, Jazz,' Jack said, more softly this time. 'You know that once an image is out there you can't get it back — or have any control over it.'

'I think that's my point,' I said lamely. My argument felt like it had returned to the beginning. 'If there weren't awful people like Tommy doing shit like that, no one would have to worry.'

'Jazz,' Jack shook his head at me, 'I love your innocence and sense of justice. I love the way you wish people were nicer, but this is reality — not that,' he pointed to the computer. 'This world is a bitch and people are even bitchier. As nice as you are, you're not going to be able to save everyone.'

And there it was. His prophecy. And he was right. I couldn't save anyone. Especially not Annie Townshend.

Post 10: Greenheadgate

Here's the post you've been waiting for — the night of Greenheadgate. I see by the number of followers and the comments that are being left that some of you are getting annoyed with the delay. But, dear reader, let me point out that this blog isn't for you. It's for me. It's for Annie. It's for Annie's parents. It's for my parents, should they ever read it, so that I can explain myself as best I can.

And now that I feel I've sufficiently set the scene leading up to Greenheadgate. It's time to break the silence we all promised to keep. It's time to finally tell the whole truth.

It started, as all good stories do, with a text message.

LILYPAD
Gathering at mine Saturday night
7pm

JAZZY
Occasion?

LILYPAD
Tommy's farewell

JAZZY
Awesome. How many?

LILYPAD
The usual suspects and sum. I'm
opening it up to Yr 10s @ Namba

JAZZY
Ooh er … that's a new idea

LILYPAD
Mixing it up with the toffees

JAZZY
Think they can handle the pace

LILYPAD
Time to bring em down to real world

JAZZY
Party Greenhead style

LILYPAD
Yeah biatches

JAZZY
Too right

The atmosphere at Namba High was electric that morning. The invite was out. Open house at Lily's and all of Year 10, Greenheads and Nambas, were invited. The response was huge. Everyone had been a bit shocked when Tommy had decided to go live with his dad south of Perth, which seemed like a million miles from Greenhead. He didn't talk about it much, except to say his mum was a bitch and he couldn't handle her anymore. To be honest, I can't say I was that upset to see him go. And I never really thought it would last — I always figured he'd be back.

'What you wearing?' Sim asked.

'I dunno. This heat is unbearable. Everything ends up sweaty and sticky.'

'Bring your bathers?' Sim suggested. I nodded. I'd just bought the cutest bikini from Tigerlily and was looking forward to wearing it.

'I think I'll wear it under those see-through shorts I just got from Iconic.'

'Get your ho on,' Sim said. I laughed. Despite my earlier protestations about the sexualisation of us, the desire to look hot conflicted badly with my feelings about the way boys treated us.

By Saturday I'd pinched three bottles of cleanskin from the winery cellar. Again, an upside of the way we lived. Alcohol was so easy for most of us to get our hands on that the children of the bakers or flower growers always dropped a few bucks cash our way — or supplied the weed they were able to grow among the wildflowers. My parents thought I was at a sleepover at Sim's, and for the record — I know I said I don't lie, but seriously, we never thought of that as lying — I was staying the night there after Lily's so I figured it was an omission, not a lie. I have since learnt there is no difference — and the legal system doesn't allow for one either.

Sim and I arrived at seven. It was still daylight — the days were so long that time of the year in Greenhead. Some blame too much daytime for the madness that ensued. But it wasn't. It was one main thing — alcohol.

The Namba kids were a bit reserved in the beginning. We owned the joint, this was our gig and our way of life and they were like the tourists that came to sample the wine.

'I like Cherry's top,' Annie said to me as we poured wine into plastic cups.

'I like yours,' I said, looking at Annie's tiny orange crop top that struggled to keep her breasts under wraps. Her red g-string sat way above her shorts.

'Do my t—' she began, but I cut her off before she could finish.

'No, they don't look huge,' I said in mock anger, 'they look sensational.'

'How are you the nicest person in the world?' she said, linking her arm through mine.

'It's hard,' I said, 'but someone has to do it.'

We drank. Lots. The Greenheads determined to show our skill and talent at partying. The Nambas loosened up and soon they were giving us a run for our money in the who-could-get-the-most-trashed stakes. Richie Lake had brought weed and the joints were being rolled thick and fast.

'Here,' Jack offered me a joint. I shook my head.

'Remember what happened at Tommy's,' I said, thinking back to the gathering about three months earlier.

'You were totally wasted,' Jack said.

'It wasn't funny,' I said, and probably made my only wise decision of the evening. 'I'll just drink.'

'Suit yourself.'

The music was up, and the dancing — if you could call it that — was happening. The boys thought it was a great game to bounce up and down as high as they could and then slam into each other. When one of them was injured they just kept going like nothing had happened. So brave. So strong. Yet, beneath it all, so afraid of the judgement of others.

When I was thrown in the pool, followed by Sim, then Lily, and Jack, Tommy and several other guys bombied in, the party was getting hectic. There was a lot of dunking and holding under water. At one point I felt like my lungs would burst and I flailed hard to punch Tommy in the nuts. When he finally let me up for breath I clung to the stonework on the side of the pool, heaving and retching. 'You're such a dick,' I spat, as water still came out of my mouth. 'You never know when to stop.'

Lily and Sim pulled me up from the edge of the pool and we posed for selfies. Sticking our boobs out, holding our bellies in. It was only later, long after Greenheadgate erupted, that I saw those photos and realised I'd had a nipple slip — something that prior to those events would have had the social media spotlight shining on me.

I found Annie in the bathroom, it must have been about ten thirty by then. I was feeling pretty pissy — but Annie was totalled. Her mascara had smudged all the way down her face. She was swaying slightly.

'What's the matter?' I asked.

'James,' she rubbed her hand under her nose, 'just dumped me.'

'Oh Annie,' I hugged her and she cried a bit more. 'Why?'

'He doesn't love me,' she pulled back and looked at me, with those big sad brown eyes. 'Why doesn't he love me, Jazz. Am I so unlovable?'

'No,' I said, wetting a washcloth, 'he's a moron.' She let me clean her up and then we went outside. It was getting really messy. I found Jack, he was so trashed.

'Jacky, you okay?' I asked, sitting next to him.

'Too. Fucked. To. Speak,' he mumbled with his eyes shut.

'I'll sit with you a bit,' I said. That was the thing about me and Jack, we always had each other's back.

Annie continued to annihilate herself. She was

with Max groping and pashing in the corner, then not much later with Liam on the couch. She was on his lap and his hand was up her skirt. Despite the fact James had left, Annie was hell-bent on proving a point. Then she staggered off to get a drink and the next time I saw her she was kind of dancing with Tommy.

I watched her collapse. Boom. Just like that. Like a sack of potatoes hitting the ground.

'Oh fuck,' I said.

Jack opened his eyes, 'What'sthematter?'

'Annie,' I pointed, 'she's wrecked.'

Jack and I made our way over to her. Tommy was crouched, patting her face lightly. 'Annie. Annie, wake up.'

She moved a hand in front of her face, brushing his aside. 'Fuck off, Tommy,' she slurred. I was relieved. She wasn't unconscious, just wasted, and she knew who we were.

'You want me to take you upstairs?' Tommy asked.

Annie nodded. 'Sure,' she mumbled.

We lifted her — Tommy, me and Jack — and carried her awkwardly up to Lily's bedroom. I arranged her into what I thought was a comfortable pose on the bed and covered her with a blanket.

'Hey,' Annie slurred, 'where's Tommy?'

'Here,' I said. Her eyes were shut.

'Tommy, stay with me,' she mumbled.

'I'll sit with her a bit,' Tommy said, 'you guys go.'

I wish I could say I wavered slightly, I wish I could say I had a bad vibe, but I didn't. I was drunk, but not enough I couldn't still party, and there was a party still going on.

'Okay, come on, Jack,' I said.

At the door Tommy called out, 'Jack, wait a sec. I need to tell you something.'

'I'll see you down there,' I said, and I shut the door behind me.

Post 11: Greenheadgate – Part 2

It's been two weeks since I last posted and I'm sorry
if that has pissed you off, dear reader. But the next
part of this story is the hardest for me to write. I
know that this is where I'll face your judgement.
And as much as this entire exercise is to truthfully
clear up the events of that night, the reality is harder
to face. I've written this post seven times. Each
time I've edited it in the hope of making it more
appealing, in order to present myself as a better
person. But the reality is, that girl, Jazz Lovely, who
wanted to be liked, who cared about others, she
changes from this point. This is where I learn things
about myself I can't ever erase.

I don't know how long Jack and Tommy were with

Annie. I'm not being cagey, it's the truth. Trust me, the police asked me plenty of times, despite the fact they had actual footage documenting most of what went on in that room. I just couldn't say. I went back down and sculling games were on. Every time someone said the word *red*, they had to drink. Because I was so drunk anyway, I was an easy target — anyone could trick me.

'What colour is Cherry's hair?'

'Red,' I'd say stupidly.

'Scull!' they'd say, pointing at my drink.

At some point Jack turned up and I do remember seeing Tommy for a bit.

'What colour g-string is Annie wearing?' I was asked.

'Red,' I said.

'Scull!' they said.

Annie.

I hadn't checked on her. We had a pact, that we would always watch each other, that if someone passed out, we would regularly check on them. How long had Annie been alone? I necked my drink and went up the stairs. The door to Lily's room was shut. I pushed it open and I remember feeling relief that, from the doorway, I could hear her snoring.

'Annie,' I whispered, moving through the darkness. The curtain was open and it was a full moon. Some say that was the reason for the madness — but it wasn't. What I saw in the moonlight confused me totally. She was face down and I remember standing there puzzling over her naked body. Why was she naked? And what was all over her skin? I pulled the curtains back further and realised with horror what had happened. She'd been drawn on, with a permanent marker. There were random squiggles over her back, but right above her arse were the words PROPERTY OF TOM and an arrow pointing down. I felt ill. I looked for her clothes. Her knickers were around her ankles and her shorts were on the floor. I rolled her over. She stirred.

'Annie,' I said, 'it's me, Jazz.' I couldn't bear to think about what had happened to her. What I saw on the other side of her body was even worse.

Across her chest in black marker were the words CHECK OUT THESE D'S. Each nipple had a ring drawn around it and MORE THAN A MOUTHFUL over each one. There were random squiggles over her torso. SLIPPERY WHEN WET written above her pubes. I thought I might vomit. I wanted to find Tommy and kill him. I guess, given how drunk I was, it had a bit of a sobering effect and this doesn't play out well for me with what I did next. I managed to lift her and pulled her top back over her head. I pulled her knickers back up and it was when I fitted her shorts over her leg that I saw the next piece of writing. Right inside her thigh had JACK WAS HERE and an arrow pointing to her vagina. It was in Jack's handwriting. At that point bile rose and I nearly puked. I picked up the black marker off the bedside table and I scrubbed out Jack's name. I scribbled over and over it until it wasn't legible. I pulled her shorts back up. She stirred again.

'Jazz,' Annie said.

'Shh,' I said, guilt twisting my gut, 'go back to sleep, Annie.' I pulled the blanket over her again.

And, like the criminal I am, I slunk from the room.

Jack was asleep with two others on the couch, in a tangle of arms and legs. I tried shaking him. I tried slapping his face. I wanted him to wake up. I needed to know what they had done. But he wouldn't wake up. I sat in the corner, hugging my knees to my chest. My phone pinged and I looked at the screen. Snapchat. It was from Callum. I opened it. It was a picture of Annie on Lily's bed, thankfully dressed, but with the permanent marker still visible over parts of her body. I released the button and let the image vanish into the ether. Then I couldn't stand it anymore. I had to get out of there. I had to go home.

I stumbled through the darkness. I was meant to be staying at Sim's but I was possessed by this overwhelming urge to go home. To get into my bed, to snuggle under my doona and hide. Forever — I hoped. Normally I'd be terrified of treading on a tiger snake but that night I didn't care. I had one mission: to get home, into bed and sleep. I guess it's the fight or flight instinct, and mine had kicked into overdrive.

Post 12: Searching for answers

The sun was streaming through my curtains when
I heard my mobile ping again. I didn't need to look
at the screen to know it was Annie. She had already
sent me five text messages. I tried to swallow but I
was so dehydrated.

> **ANNIE**
> **Jazz!**

> **ANNIE**
> **Wake up**

> **ANNIE**
> **Jazz! Jazz! WAKE UP!**

> **ANNIE**
> **Text me ASAP**

> **ANNIE**
> **What the fuck happened to me last night**

I read her words again and again, my fingers hovering over the keypad. I didn't know how much to tell her. I didn't know how to word the text. My hands were shaking. I tried to delay — I know it sounds callous, but there were items sitting in my Snapchat. I had to know how far this had gone before I replied to her. I opened the images, and they were all from Tommy. They were all of Annie undressed, with different stages of graffiti drawn over her. The images made me shudder, particularly the one with Jack between her legs drawing on her thigh. I squeezed my eyes shut but in the cold light of day everything was even worse than it had been the night before. More obscene.

JAZZY
You drank way too much and passed out

It was a pathetic response. I knew that. But how do you send someone a text telling them they've been drawn on and humiliated by guys they've known for years? Guys they consider their friends? How do you tell them there are photos of it circulating already?

ANNIE
Jazz I'm totally freaking out here. I'm covered in fucking black pen. What happened to me?

I squinted against the sun and the tears. I just couldn't type it. Some conversations are not meant for text. I tapped the call button. She picked up immediately.

'Jazz?' Annie's voice was soft and pained.

'Annie,' I didn't know what to say.

'What fucking happened?' Annie whispered. I paused and looked out the window. It was such a beautiful day yet everything felt so ugly.

'We put you to bed,' I began really softly. 'You had totally crashed out. And Tommy said he'd sit with you for a bit. I left you there and when I came back later you were naked and drawn on.' I know I was omitting the photos, but it seemed impossible to hit her with everything straight away.

'Did Tommy do this?' Annie whispered. 'Who is we?'

'Tommy, Jack and me put you to bed,' I said and then I rushed on quickly. 'It was Tommy and Jack who drew on you.'

'Jack?' Annie's voice rose hysterically, then broke.

'Why the fuck would Jack do this to me?'

I squeezed my eyes tightly shut. 'I don't know, Annie. They were drunk. They were being stupid.' It sounded so lame and so much like collusion.

'What else?' she demanded more firmly now. 'The shit they wrote on me, Jazz. Did they ... did they ...' She couldn't finish the question.

'No!' I said firmly. Did they what? Touch her? Rape her? 'Jack would never allow anything like that to happen. But they photographed you,' I said. The howl that came out of her throat sounded like an animal dying.

'Have you seen them?' she asked finally.

'Yes,' I said in a monotone.

'Oh fuck,' she was barely comprehensible. 'And?'

'Six pictures,' I said, each image graphically etched into my memory. 'All of you naked, with various stages of writing on you.'

'Have you got them?' she asked quietly.

'No,' I hurried to add, 'they were sent on Snapchat. They're gone now.'

'You didn't screenshot them?'

'It was only three seconds, I think.'

'Who sent them?' Annie asked.

'Tommy.' I squeezed my eyes shut — I knew where this was going.

'He's sent them to everyone,' Annie said flatly. 'Why? Why? Why?' Annie struggled to speak. 'Why would they fucking do that to me? Oh fuck. My life is over.'

'It's not,' I hurried, 'it'll blow over. It'll be forgotten soon.' It sounded like total bullshit to my own ears.

'I've gotta go,' Annie said suddenly. 'I'll talk to you later.' And then she hung up. How on earth was this ever going to be forgotten?

Thankfully my parents were out when I slipped down the hallway over the cool slate tiles to the bathroom. I stripped off last night's clothes and as the shower heated up I assessed myself in the mirror. How would Annie have felt when she woke up in Lily's bed, disoriented? Then when she took her clothes off and saw the drawings all over her body. I imagine she searched her brain — for one tiny memory — and got nothing. Just total blackness. Now to know she'd been stripped and looked at, photographed and now looked at again — by who? By how many? I stood under the hot spray and scrubbed hard at my own skin, as if it too was covered in permanent marker.

By the time I was dressed and in front of my laptop the news was already on Facebook.

Post 13: What a mofo ho

That was the title of the first Facebook post (and there were many to follow) that marked the beginning of Greenheadgate. It was accompanied by one of the pictures of Annie, naked, face down and drawn all over. It had more than 200 Likes when I first saw it — but I believe by the time Annie couldn't take it anymore the number was over a thousand. It was the comments that made my skin crawl.

> **Saw the ho with several dudes before then, horny mutherfucker**
>
> **Woah dirty little slut**
>
> **When drunk girls act like sluts**
>
> **Who is that filthy bitch**
>
> **Great arse**
>
> **Slutty ho**

... and so on — you get the idea. Again, the thing that was disturbing (apart from the entire thing) was that the comments were written by both girls and guys. Nowhere, not once on that first morning, did anyone defend Annie. I had been drunk and abandoned her. I had left her in the hands of two drunk guys. She had been drunk and passed out. How was what she had done so bad? Why weren't people hanging shit on Tommy and Jack? Why was Annie not the victim here? Why was Annie the dirty slut who got what was coming?

I defended her.

> **You people make me sick. You blame a girl who is UNCONSCIOUS. Who does not give her consent to be photographed, let alone stripped and violated. How is she to blame? How is she at fault? How is it okay to say the victim of a crime is responsible?**

And the responses came thick and fast.

> **She was drunk and asked for it**
>
> **She asked for it**
>
> **She was acting like a slut before then. I was there I saw her.**
>
> **I was there and hooked up with her**
>
> **Me too**
>
> **Me three**

Great tits

Horny bitch

**If you are going to trash yourself
and pass out then you get what you
deserve**

And that last comment came from a girl from
Namba High. I sat in my room shaking. No one saw
this from Annie's perspective. They all blamed her. I
thought back to when she was hooking up with the
other guys. She was out of control, definitely. She
was being a bit slutty. But the difference was she was
making those choices (as limited as her decision-
making ability was). At least she was consenting
to it. Wasn't that the difference? Whether you give
consent or not?

A chat window opened in the bottom corner.

**ANNIE TOWNSHEND
Fuck Jazz, this is already out of control**

**JASMINE LOVELY
I know but it's just news at the min.
It'll pass**

**ANNIE TOWNSHEND
I contacted Tommy—he says he
deleted them**

**JASMINE LOVELY
Phew**

ANNIE TOWNSHEND
You don't fucking believe him do
you?

JASMINE LOVELY
It was on Snapchat

ANNIE TOWNSHEND
Taken on Tommy's phone. And now
this one's on FB???

JASMINE LOVELY
What do you want to do?

ANNIE TOWNSHEND
I need to see them. I need them
deleted

JASMINE LOVELY
If you want I'll contact Tommy

I waited, but she wasn't typing a response. I
didn't know what to do. Should I contact Tommy
and ask him to send them, so she could see them?
Why would she want to see them? But then I figured
if other people had seen them she would want to
see them, too. I made up my mind: I'd make Tommy
give me those photos even if I had to smash the
shit out of him. Before I could message him, Annie
responded.

ANNIE TOWNSHEND
Don't bother

JASMINE LOVELY
What? Why?

ANNIE TOWNSHEND
I've seen them

JASMINE LOVELY
Tommy?

ANNIE TOWNSHEND
No, they've been sent to me three
times

JASMINE LOVELY
Fuck

ANNIE TOWNSHEND
People are the fucking worst

JASMINE LOVELY
I'm so sorry

ANNIE TOWNSHEND
My reputation is totally ruined and I
can't even remember what happened

JASMINE LOVELY
I don't know what to say

ANNIE TOWNSHEND
Nuthin. I'm a fucking ho. That's it
now. Gotta go. I'll talk to you later

JASMINE LOVELY
<3

The rest of the day I spent in my room. The
pictures were sent to me again and again. There

were more updates on Facebook and Tommy was inviting people to message him for details. By details he meant more photos. Or at least that's what I thought then. It didn't seem like much worse could come out. I messaged Jack.

JASMINE LOVELY
Make him stop

JACK WEST
I keep telling him but he's out of control

JASMINE LOVELY
This is totally fucked. Annie is freaking out. I can't believe what you did. I'm disgusted with you

JACK WEST
I'm really embarrassed. I'm really sorry. I texted Annie. I just don't remember any of it. I can't believe those photos are real

JASMINE LOVELY
Why would you do that to her?

JACK WEST
I guess it was just meant to be a joke. Something funny. People do it all the time. You know that

JASMINE LOVELY
Are you for serious? You draw a penis on their face. You don't draw on their fucking genitals

JACK WEST
We went too far

JASMINE LOVELY
WTF? Is there something else?

JACK WEST
What?

JASMINE LOVELY
Did something else happen?

JACK WEST
FFS. I didn't mean that. I meant what
we did was too far. You know me,
you know I wouldn't do any shit like
that

JASMINE LOVELY
I don't know what to think anymore.
I don't even know who you are

He didn't reply to me for ages. And then after a while
I saw he had gone offline. I felt angry that he had
ignored me. How dare he? He was the wrongdoer,
not me. He should be begging my forgiveness. I'd
been harsh with him, but he totally deserved it. His
behaviour had been disgusting. You just don't do shit
like that to your friends and think it's funny.

Post 14: The video

For those of you from Greenhead and Namba,
you've seen the photos. In fact, you've probably
seen the video too. You know what happened in
that bedroom. And while I'm wary of perpetuating
it here, I know that all the footage eventually went
viral, when this all came out. I'm mindful, now, of
the damage that the internet can cause, so at the
risk of using the internet to further compound the
pain and misery that footage caused to everyone,
but particularly Annie, I'm being cautious in how I
recount what happened next.

I had just dozed off — it must have been nearly 1 am
— but as tired and as hung-over as I was I couldn't
stop my racing brain. This was turning explosive

and Annie was about to face all the fallout from the gathering. I would've hated to be her that night. I wondered if she would be at the bus stop for school in the morning.

There was a tapping at my window. At first I hoped it was the wind, a branch knocking against the glass. But it was insistent and followed with, 'Jazz, wake up. Wake up.'

I sat up and pulled the curtain back. Jack's white face appeared in the moonlight. 'Let me in, something terrible has happened.'

My heart was thundering in my chest. What terrible thing had happened? What thing more terrible than the last terrible thing could have Jack at my window?

He was out of breath and trembling as he landed on my bed. His hands were shaking as he offered me his phone.

'I'm in so much trouble,' he said, and he was trying not to cry. 'What the fuck have I done?'

I couldn't take my eyes off him. He sat there with his head bowed, his lip trembling. This had to be bad. I looked at the phone. Tapped on Messages and watched the video Tommy had sent Jack. Lily's room wavered on the screen. Jack is the cameraman, he zooms in on Annie lying under the blanket (you'll remember the one I pulled over her, twice). Tommy appears in the shot holding up the marker.

'Now, what do we want to say?' Jack makes a muffled noise, maybe a laugh, and Tommy pulls her top over her head. 'Fuck me,' Tommy says, staring at Annie's boobs. He starts writing. Jack laughs. It sickens me. 'Your turn,' Tommy offers him the pen. The camera is swapped, it films the ceiling and then Jack is writing across the lower part of Annie's abdomen. The camera changes hands again. Tommy pulls her shorts off, pulls her knickers down, laughs again. It's vile and awful. I don't want to watch, but I have this feeling creeping over me, that there is more than just the writing.

The next thing Tommy does makes me look away. He turns her over, he writes those words over her arse and then, he sticks his fingers in her. It is the most disgusting thing I've ever seen. I think I retch.

The camera is now filming the ceiling but there is noise recorded. Grunting, laughter, Tommy's voice, 'Come on, Jack, your turn.' The camera shifts back to Annie, she's on her back now, her eyes are shut and as it moves down her body, zooming in on her nipples, there's Jack. He's pulling his fingers out of her and writing on the inside of her leg.

The screen goes black.

'You're disgusting,' I spat. I never thought Jack was capable of this — I thought the writing on her, the stripping of her, was beyond comprehension. But he assaulted her. He raped her.

Jack looked like shit. His hair was a mess and he had the darkest rings under his eyes. His skin had a slightly greenish hue to it. I felt ill to my very core. It felt like my nervous system was going into total shutdown.

'Jazz,' Jack said. But I couldn't look at him. I stared out of the window, the phone still held limply in my hand. What had he done? I couldn't get it straight in my head. What had they done? I couldn't speak.

'Jazz,' Jack whispered, 'say something.'

But what could I say? It'll be alright, Jack? It'll blow over? This would never be alright. I didn't know what to do, or say.

'Jazz, are you ever going to speak to me again?'

'I don't know,' I couldn't meet his eyes. The sound of his voice made me cringe. I wanted him to get out of my room. I wanted this to all go away. 'I don't think I can ever like you ever again.'

'Jazz,' he pleaded, 'I don't think I can live if you won't speak to me.' His voice was muffled in his hands. 'I've done the worst thing ever, but it was a mistake, a drunk and stupid mistake.'

'You raped her,' I cried, finally looking at him. 'You're a rapist.'

'No,' he shook his head from side to side, 'no.' That's when he started sobbing. Heart-wrenching, gut-heaving sobs. He gagged a few times. I watched him coldly. And then I saw ten-year-old Jack. My best friend. The boy who'd kicked Nathan Reilly in the nuts for grabbing my boob, the boy who taught me how to rollerblade and waterski, the boy who came and sat on my bed when I got my first period and brought me pads, the boy who wrapped his arms around me and curled into me when my heart was broken after Scottie McGough hooked up with Lisa Temple when we were going out together, the boy who I'd always believed would be my best friend forever. My Jacky boy.

And here, dear reader, is where I fear I'll lose you forever. This is what I did next. I looked at Jack, my best friend Jack, who had just gang-raped one of my other best friends, and then I crossed the room, crouched in front of him and put my arms around him. This time, I held him when his heart was broken.

'Who has Tommy sent that to?' I nodded towards Jack's phone.

'I don't know,' he said. 'He knows not to spread it. He must know that this looks bad for him and me.'

And then it dawned on me. And suddenly I knew what was about to happen. 'You don't get it, Jack,' I spoke to him wearily. 'You don't see how Tommy sees things. This is a conquest for him. This is a step up from Casey's boobs, and the graffitied body of Annie. This makes Tommy look like the big man. This is going to get out.'

Jack shook his head. 'No, I don't think he'll do that. It was a stupid prank that went too far.'

'Too far?' I shouted. I wanted to punch his face in. 'Rape is more than just too far!'

'He won't,' Jack said firmly. 'I know Tommy

better than you. He's all bullshit, talking big-man crap. He won't incriminate himself.'

'Really,' I said, so, so sarcastically. And I crossed my room to my dresser and picked my phone up, because if there was one thing I was sure of it was that the video was sitting there in my Messages. The app had the red number 1 over it. I tapped it and watched Lily's bedroom come into focus. 'He already has,' I held the phone up to Jack.

Post 15: The apocalypse

I went back to bed after Jack had crawled out my window and gone home, but I got no sleep. My brain was still racing. I couldn't control it. I couldn't get what I'd seen on that screen out of my head, and it made me sick. I lay in bed, slightly trembling, waiting for the sun to rise. Not knowing what to do. What would I say to Annie? What shit would happen next?

Annie was waiting for us at the bus stop as Jack and I arrived at the same time. It felt like the apocalypse and we were the walking dead. I couldn't look at her but the moment Jack's dark-circled, puffy eyes met mine I knew what I had to do. No matter what happened, I had to show Annie the video before we got on the school bus.

'Hey,' she was trying to be upbeat. It was admirable.

'How are you?' I asked, finally making eye contact.

'I'm here,' she said flatly, and stared coldly at Jack.

'Annie,' Jack started, but his voice broke and his lip trembled. 'I'm so, so, so sorry.'

'Yeah.' She wouldn't look at him. She hated him, and things were just about to get so much worse. She had to see that video before we got on the bus.

'Annie.' I watched the orange bus pull out of the Walkers' winery. 'There's a video.'

'What?' the colour drained immediately from her face.

'It's bad,' I said.

'Show it to me,' she held her hand out. The bus was about two-hundred metres away. I gave her the phone. She watched it quickly, she didn't even flinch, then handed it back to me. The bus doors opened. Jack looked at me. I waved him on. There was no way I was leaving her. I'd wag school with her. We'd talk, figure this shit out.

She made to get on the bus.

'Wait,' I put a hand on her arm, 'other people may have it.'

She was on the step above me and looked down. 'I figured that. So what? There's nothing there they haven't seen already,' she said flatly.

'But there is,' I was holding the bus up. Al, the bus driver, called at me. 'On or off, Miss Lovely. Make it quick.'

'It shows ...' I couldn't finish the sentence.

'Jack and Tommy raping me,' Annie said through tears. 'Maybe now people will believe I'm not such a whore.'

I followed her onto the bus and couldn't look at Jack as we walked past him to the back seat.

Post 16: No excuses for girls gone wild

So the first day at school was relatively calm. All the gossip and snide remarks were regarding the photos. I walked with Annie down the hallways, watching the guys huddle over their phones. It was really strange, but knowing there was something worse out there made those photos seem insignificant. It was easy to act like Casey had — defiantly. We — Annie, Jack and me — knew exactly what was on that video. We just didn't know who had seen it or had it in their possession. Jack was our best chance of finding out, but by lunchtime he knew nothing more.

'No one has mentioned it,' Jack told me. 'Everyone is only talking about the photos. Maybe I was right after all. Tommy knows how bad this is for the both of us. Maybe he only sent it to me and you.'

I shook my head in disbelief. 'Just doesn't fit with his MO. Is he at his dad's?'

'Guess so,' Jack shrugged, 'he was meant to leave yesterday. He hasn't replied to any of my texts. Maybe he feels bad about it.'

I may have snorted. 'That would imply he cared — or had an ounce of compassion in his body. I don't think so. This is his final hand grenade.'

By the time the buses were arriving to take us home, I was starting to believe that the worst thing that was going to happen was Annie facing those photos. Dealing with that reputation. And when I assessed it like that it wasn't anywhere near as bad as what we had feared. It would blow over, like it did for Casey. We were defiant enough — we could carry it off. We could face them all — the slut-shamers — and just be like, 'Whatever. So what? I don't care.' But this time, actually and truly mean it. Maybe — and I guess at this point I was getting a bit fanciful — our defiance would take the sting out of this kind of shit. That if other girls saw how Annie handled those pictures, if other girls saw that Annie was so 'in-your-face, I don't give a flying fuck', then maybe it would end this kind of terrorism. And terrorism might sound like an exaggeration, but that is what it was. It took bullying to a new level. Gone were the days when you lived in fear of what someone could do to you. Now you lived in fear of your worst mistakes being paraded around the globe to take you down. And there was no defence because 'you asked for it'. Well, maybe there was. Maybe we had unwittingly stumbled on an end to social and emotional terrorism. If there was nowhere for it to land — then it had no effect. Right?

Sometimes optimism has no place in this world.

Despite feeling so positive about the video never emerging, the sledging on Facebook increased overnight and into the next day. The picture of Annie face-down with Tommy's obscenity written above her arse had been tagged to people beyond Namba. There were two guys in particular who made the most offensive comments and received the most Likes and responses. These two guys were getting off on the celebrity that Annie's picture was giving them.

BEN RITCHIE
My anaconda don't... Likes: 234

DAMO MILLS
**Looks like Tom's anaconda does!
Likes: 256**

Underneath each of their comments was another whole thread of comments. It was like a pyramid scheme. I clicked on their profiles—both were set to private and there was nothing much to see. Two average guys, who didn't know Annie and were just making fun of a random picture. Suzie Quinn was another commenter who caught my attention. She was full of such hate.

SUZIE QUINN
**That dirty slut makes me sick. Total
whorebag. Likes: 124**

Her profile was also private, but she had a lot of profile pics visible to the public. I scrolled through them. Mostly selfies—no great surprise there. But one caught my eye—a typical bathroom selfie with Suzie Quinn in her underwear. Big deal, right? There were girls in our school as young as Year 7 who had posted pictures like that. I wouldn't have thought anything of it except for her vitriol. Who got to set the parameters for what made you a whore or not? Underwear versus bathers, topless versus top, passed out and dressed versus passed out and violated? It was truly sickening.

Annie texted me.

ANNIE
It's out of control

JAZZY
Who are these people

ANNIE
Fk

JAZZY
Something else will happen. It'll die down soon

ANNIE
I guess. What if it's the video?

JAZZY
It wont be

ANNIE
Im not sure

JAZZY
Remember it makes Tommy and Jack look like criminals

ANNIE
Because they are

JAZZY
Soz. I know. That's what I meant

ANNIE
Still hope it doesn't come out. It
makes me feel sick

JAZZY
Me too

And here's the thing. It made me really sick. I
know this will make the haters comment on my post
but I'll state it anyway. I was worried for Annie, but
also Jack. What would happen to him if this went
public? Could he be charged with rape? What about
his future, if he was labelled a sex offender?

Post 17: Viral

Thank you for the multitude of comments regarding my concerns for Jack. It is very easy with the power of hindsight to see how better to handle things. Unfortunately, at the time I was dealing with things as they happened. My concerns were for two of my friends, my best friend Annie (who had been the victim of a crime) and my other best friend Jack (who had been one of the perpetrators). As for Tommy — I'd just as soon spit on him. I know Jack was guilty but it was easy to blame this all on Tommy. Tommy who had, since the party and the dissemination of the pictures, conveniently vanished.

   The photos had gone further by the next day. It was constant — phones being passed, smirks, laughter and exclamations. I don't know how Annie handled it, but she did. People say that Annie took the coward's way by doing what she did in the end, but Annie was no coward. That week I watched her bravely endure the taunts and hate from kids at school. I know that every night she sat there on Facebook reading and watching the comments. And every day she got up, got dressed and went to school. I know she couldn't concentrate. I know she wasn't really present. She was just there physically, but mentally she was back at Lily's place, not drinking herself into a coma. She was waiting patiently for this to blow over and be replaced by something else. Four days after the party, it was. The video went viral.

We were sitting in Chemistry. I watched Jacob nudge Liam and pass his phone under the desk. Liam mouthed the words 'What the fuck' and passed it to Scott. Scott's face was sheer shock. He shook his head, and the phone was passed to Jack. Jack went white. Looked up to see me staring at him. I involuntarily shook my head, he involuntarily nodded, we both involuntarily looked at Annie. She was near the front, head down, trying to pretend she was working out some irrelevant chemical equation. My phone vibrated. I slid it out of my pocket.

JACKY
It's on Tommy's FB

I felt sick. I opened Facebook. The video was there. It started autoplaying on my newsfeed, silently. I texted Annie.

JAZZY
It's on Tommy's FB

I watched her. She couldn't get her phone out of her pocket as Mr Daniels was near her. She waited for him to move off. She looked at her phone for the longest time. It occurred to me she was watching the video again. She didn't turn, she started texting. She didn't see Mr Daniels approach.

'Miss Townshend, I must assume that is a phone in your lap, as I can't imagine your lap is so interesting it can hold your total attention.'

'I wouldn't be too sure, sir,' Liam shouted out. Annie's head spun around so fast I thought she would have whiplash. Her face was white, with two bright red blotches.

'From all accounts it's pretty interesting,' Jacob

added. Mr Daniels squinted at them.

'That's enough,' he stated and looked at Annie. 'Phone away or I'll take it.' Annie stood up. 'Miss Townshend?' Mr Daniels frowned.

'I need to go to the bathroom, sir,' she said quietly. She didn't wait for his reply, she left the room.

When the class ended she still hadn't returned to collect her books. I raced to the toilets, no sign of her anywhere. I texted and called. No response. She didn't appear at lunchtime. She didn't come to Maths. I wondered where she was, although I figured she must have gone home. I can't say I blamed her. It was on Facebook, it was open to the whole world.

I kept texting Annie, but she didn't reply. She didn't make her presence known on Facebook or Snapchat or Instagram. Shots had been fired and she had vanished.

Post 18: Judas

I was really tired. I'd been up all night immersed in the chat. The tone had changed. Annie was no longer the subject of all the hate. In fact, a huge contingent of girls from school had come out in support of her. The Soul Sisters, girls at school whose mums were like the Real Housewives of Greenhead, led the charge to defend Annie.

TASH HIGGINS
This is a disgusting video. You boys should be ashamed of yourselves. How could you? Please remove this video immediately.

NAOMI MATHERS
You are disrespectful and revolting. Your treatment of that poor girl is horrendous. I've never seen anything as vile in my life. Please remove this.

LOZ JONES
You criminals. Rapists. You
disgusting sick animals.

CHARLIE BETTS
You should be reported to the
police. Annie honey, I'm so sorry this
happened to you.

LOULOU MCCARTNEY
Tommy you are an animal. Jack I'm
horrified by you. You make me sick. I
hope you get arrested.

Our immediate group was less diplomatic.

SIM LAWRENCE
What the fuck? Take this fucking
thing down. Annie inbox me.

LILY PHILLIPS
Is this for serious. I can't believe
it. What the fuck are you thinking
Tommy? Jack? WTF?? Annie inbox me.

And the comments just kept coming.

Pigs

Perverts

Vile and filthy animals

Jail is too good for you

Castration anyone?

As far as I know, Annie remained silent that night,

and she wasn't the only one. It was noted that I hadn't commented. I, Jazz Lovely, Annie's best friend. The view was that my lack of contribution showed I was clearly on the wrong side. Everyone thought I was in the boys' camp — why else wouldn't I go on a vitriolic rampage too? In light of what happened later, this ended up looking very bad for me too. But the truth was, I didn't know what to say. I wanted to respond, but I just couldn't. I'd seen the video, seen what Jack had done, but there was a tiny part of me that hoped it wasn't exactly that. That it was a trick of the camera, the lighting. It sounds pathetic when I write it now. But I just didn't want to condemn Jack, I didn't want to publicly side against him. I just wanted it all to stop.

As the night progressed, the readership widened. Friends who Liked the video had their friends Liking it too. Tommy had set the privacy on the post to 'public'. Despite the fact the original post was removed by Facebook, the video kept reappearing on other people's timelines. It had a momentum that was terrifying. By midnight there were schools as far away as Albany commenting. And the further from Greenhead the comments came, the more hatred they contained — mostly towards Annie. Guys making comments about chicks in the country, how boring life must be out there, asking how to get invited to a gathering, that kind of crap. One guy, Baz something, kept beefing it up. Commenting in his virtually illiterate way on every single post, it got to the point where people finally ignored him until he shut up. But it was horrific, as if what had happened to Annie wasn't the worst thing ever, it was being multiplied a thousand times. All these people getting their fifteen minutes of fame — at Annie's expense.

And then Tommy made contact.

> **TOM ROBINSON**
> **You people need to lighten up. It's not criminal. She wanted it.**

The responses (and I think there were over two hundred) mostly contained the sentiment 'nice one rapist'. It didn't stop Tommy.

> **TOM ROBINSON**
> **For the record, it was consensual.**

The responses to that drew attention to the fact that Annie was clearly unconscious during the attack. It also drew comments from Tommy's friends who defended him, labelled Annie a slut and referenced her behaviour earlier in the night. James the ex-boyfriend weighed in.

> **JAMES MITCHELL**
> **I went out with her for six months. I had no idea she was such a ho. What she was doing at the party shows that she did want it. Don't blame Tommy, if anyone is at fault it was Annie. I can't believe I went there. She is disgusting.**

I couldn't believe him. James had sunk the boot in big time. He rallied the troops with his comment, and Tommy and his mates seized on it.

> **TOM ROBINSON**
> **Cheers bro. Now I see why you dumped her. Can't keep her legs shut.**

And on it went again.

It was truly a nightmare.

I was not surprised when neither Annie nor Jack was at the bus stop in the morning. I texted Jack on the way to school.

> **JAZZY**
> **Where r u?**

> **JACKY**
> **In bed. Sick. Really fucking sick.**

JAZZY
Seriously?

JACKY
I can't face it. The hate.

JAZZY
I know

But seriously? He couldn't face the hate? Before when it was Annie, alone, everyone was pretty fine with it all. But now Jack had to disappear because he was the target of their hate and derision? It was hard to comprehend. In fact, most things are hard to comprehend, until it's you.

Annie surprised us all by turning up late to first class. We were in Food Tech and she came in, tying her apron and pulling her long brown hair back into a ponytail.

'Hey,' I said as I got the ingredients from the central table. 'You okay?'

She blanked me. She gathered her ingredients and moved to her bench. I frowned. What else could have happened between the video and now — aside from the haters hating? Surely Annie could see that she had some support — as minimal as it was? I didn't have to wait long to find out what Annie's new source of angst was. Jack texted me.

JACKY
Tommy's FB NOW

I excused myself from class and ran to the toilets. The connection was slow and I sat in the putrid toilets waiting for the page to load.

The post came up. I died.

Dear reader, please forgive me for the lapse in memory — but it wasn't until that moment, and seeing those photos, that I remembered. Sitting in the toilets looking at them on my phone, I suddenly remembered *exactly* what had happened. A black spot in my memory had been visually filled. I felt cold and then hot. I struggled to breathe. I pulled my hair off my neck and gasped for breath.

The post read: HOT CHICK ON CHICK ACTION. And there was me, cupping Annie's boobs and sticking my tongue in her ear.

We put her on the bed, her top lifts up and her boobs are poking out. I try to wrestle them back in. There is a flash and I turn to see Tommy holding up his iPhone.

'Awesome girl on girl action,' he says.

I don't know why, but it seems funny and I laugh.
I prop Annie's head on my shoulder and pose for
Tommy's camera. Then Tommy says, 'Show us your
tits, Jazz.' I untie my string bikini and let it drop.

'They're hardly tits,' he says, snapping away on
his phone. And I don't know why I do it, I'm awash
with some type of jealousy, but I say, 'You want tits,
Tommy?' And I lift up Annie's top, cup her boobs and
make out like I am kissing her ear. 'How about them
then?' I say.

'She's got fantastic tits,' Tommy leers.

I pull her top back down and lay her on the bed.
'Annie, you okay?' I ask. She kind of grunts, so I get a
light blanket and cover her. Then I leave.

I grappled with the images before me. I did that?
I couldn't believe it — but I had. I'd treated her
like a piece of meat. A drunk, passed-out girl. I'd
manhandled her, touched her, abused her. My own
friend.

I bowed my head in shame. No, in horror. And
I remembered it. I know, dear reader, you are
reeling at this revelation of me — me, the would-
be campaigner for girls, the one who seemingly

defended my friend in her hour of need. But I was reeling more. To be faced with such images of yourself, acting like someone else, was horrific. In that toilet stall I remembered everything. It had seemed harmless. A joke. Propping her up and doing that. But to the sober Jazz Lovely, who was in class with the victim of her abuse? It was more than horrific. How could I have done that? What on earth was I thinking? Buoyed by booze? Fuelled by Tommy? I was sick, sick to my very stomach. I actually gagged. And here is what I did: exactly what the others had done before me. I walked out of that toilet and vanished. I couldn't face anyone. Let alone Annie.

I ignored her texts.

> **ANNIE**
> **Why? Why? I thought we were friends**
>
> **ANNIE**
> **Jazz reply to me**
>
> **ANNIE**
> **You owe me that**
>
> **ANNIE**
> **I fucking hate you**

I sat in my bedroom watching each text bling on

my screen. And I did nothing. I never responded to her. In the light of what happened next, I wish I had been a better person. I abused her, but then, even worse, I abandoned her.

Post 19: Confessions

Thank you, dear reader, for your comments of both encouragement and vitriol. I deserve everything I get. I'm not looking for sympathy. This is, according to Greek theatre, what catharsis is. The release of emotion. An attempt to make sense of the horror. And that is what I'm doing — I have no other choice. Because after I was revealed as Judas, after I betrayed Annie three times, things got so much worse. More than any of us in our little insular Greenhead community could ever have imagined.

That next day, I had to face the masses. Their judgement, their hatred. While Annie was being labelled a slut, she was the target. Then Jack and Tommy, the rapists. But I was about to be hit with the worst of it. I know it sounds like me, me, me. But this was what I was about to face. The one thing you can be sure about haters is that they love to hate. And give them something out of the norm — they'll find a way to hate it more. I couldn't shake the images. I'd stayed up all night on Facebook. I'd watched the mud slinging, the things they were saying about me. 'Dog act.' I knew Annie had been watching too, and Jack, and Tommy — from his protected little hidey-hole. All of us, alone in our rooms, yet spectators at the same show. It was unavoidable. I couldn't escape the confrontation and there was no point in delaying it further. I had to go and face them. Face Annie.

Annie wasn't at the bus stop in the morning and my heart sank. What if she didn't turn up? Then I had put myself out there for nothing. I shrugged, it didn't matter anyway — this wasn't something I could run from forever. She was making a habit of missing the bus — I could only wonder what she was telling her parents to get them to drive her in each day. I sat at the back of the bus with my headphones on. Jack was still absent and though I'd thought he was such a coward before, now I really understood why he couldn't face anyone.

When I arrived at school, I was surprised by the lack of interest in me. Sure, there were a few looks, guys sharing their phones around. But what was the point in worrying if the images were of me feeling Annie up? Everyone had seen them. I just had to find Annie and apologise.

The hallways were quiet. It was like today was a rostered day off for most students. I walked to home room. Where was everyone? I put my bag in my locker and Mr Taylor, the Dean of Year 10, came by.

'There is a full-school assembly in the gym, Miss Lovely,' he said. I know I was in a full state of paranoia, but did he look at me disapprovingly? Did he know what had happened? Why was there an unscheduled assembly? As I neared the gym I heard the voices of the school, but again, it sounded different to normal, not as raucous, not as loud. It sounded subdued.

'What's going on?' I asked Paige, a girl from my homeroom. Her eyes flashed something, I don't know what — disgust?

'Not sure,' she said, 'but some shit's gone down.' And then I wasn't being paranoid — she turned her back on me. I moved into the gym with the others and sat in the Year 10 section. No Jack. No Annie. No Tommy. I was the guilty party without a party. I hugged my knees. The principal stood behind the lectern.

'We have a very grave situation unfolding here at Namba High School,' he said, and my heart sank. This was about the party, the pictures, the rape. Annie. 'The relevant authorities have been called and parents are being notified.' I saw them all look my way. At that point I wished I was dead. I hugged my knees tighter. 'Annie Townshend attempted to commit suicide last night.' And then my ears went deaf. I couldn't hear the words he was saying. I watched his mouth moving, but I couldn't hear a thing. Annie had attempted to kill herself. Annie was dead? Or wasn't? I got to my feet. Every head in the gym turned my way. But I moved to the side and looked at Mr Stock. 'Toilet,' I mouthed. He shook his head, indicating I should sit back down, but I couldn't. I ignored him. Walked straight past him and outside. I collapsed onto one of the benches. I had to get out. But then there was a hand on my shoulder. It was Miss Jones, the school psych

'Jasmine?' she said. I looked at her and I couldn't speak. 'Come to my office.'

I sat on her couch and stared numbly at her.

'What happened?' I asked finally. She put a box of tissues on the round table in front of me.

'Annie is your friend.' It wasn't a question. But I shook my head.

'No,' I said. 'She hates me.'

Miss Jones looked perplexed. 'You had a fight?'

I nodded. 'What did she do?' I asked.

'I don't want to go into the details,' Miss Jones said, 'but she tried to end her life. Her mother prevented it. She's in hospital.'

I sighed, but it came out as a sob. 'She's not dead. She's not dead.' I couldn't believe it. For those few minutes I thought she was dead. I thought we had killed her. It was an enormous relief. The burden had lifted.

'She's not dead,' Miss Jones said, and then she grasped my hand. She said very softly, 'She's in a very bad way, Jasmine. She's on life support. It doesn't look good.'

And then that burden fell straight back over me. Oh God. What had we done? 'I'm in real trouble,'

I said without looking at Miss Jones. 'I've done something bad.' She nodded and passed me a tissue.

'The school is aware of some circumstances leading to this situation. But what do you know, Jasmine? What can you tell me?'

I shook my head. 'I can't tell you.' I realised that if I said anything they would go after Jack. Tommy could die for all I cared — he had no remorse. But Jack. And what about me? My part in it?

'I had a fight with her and ignored her last night.' I started crying. It wasn't as if that was my only crime, or even my worst one. But at that point it was the only thing on my mind. If I had responded to her messages, maybe she wouldn't have done this. 'I need my mum,' I said. Miss Jones nodded.

'I'll call her,' she reached for the phone. 'Jasmine,' she said as she punched in the numbers, 'it's all going to come out. Mr Fletcher is going to want to speak to you.'

I nodded, but there was no way I was talking to the principal, or anyone else, until I had spoken to my mum and dad.

Post 20: A mother's disappointment

The thing about parents is they can shout at you, ground you, take away your phone and internet, make you do chores, but when they say 'I'm so disappointed in you' it's a killer. It cuts deep, worse than anything else — or so I thought. My parents didn't even utter those words. My mum just cried and cried, and my dad, well, he didn't even come to the interview. After, my dad wouldn't look at me. I knew then that something was broken forever.

'What's happened?' Mum asked as she rushed through the door of Miss Jones' office. I looked at Miss Jones, who stood up.

'I'll leave you two,' she said, closing the door behind her.

'Jazz,' Mum sat opposite me, 'talk to me. You're scaring me.'

I sniffed and wiped my eyes. 'Things have got out of control.'

'Things, what things?' Mum sounded panicked.

'A party, last week,' I said.

'Whose party?' Mum ran a hand through her hair. I wasn't making this easy for her to follow, but the real words I needed to say were blocking my throat.

'At Lily's,' I said.

'Were you there?' Mum frowned.

'Yes,' I nodded, facing the first glint of disappointment in her eyes. 'I told you I was staying the night at Sim's but I went to a party instead.'

Mum sighed, 'Oh Jazz, what happened?'

'It got a bit out of hand. We got pretty drunk.'

'You? You got drunk?'

I thought, you haven't even heard the half of it.

'Not just me, everyone. Annie the worst.' Suddenly the words started rushing. 'She passed out. She got drawn on and she got ...' I gasped for air, 'drawn on with texta and then she got ... touched, by some boys.'

'What?' Mum shook her head. 'What?'

'They touched her,' I pointed to my own body — I couldn't say those words to my mother. It was like we were a bunch of depraved perverts — which I was realising we had been — but I couldn't say the words 'they fingered her' to my own mother. It made me shudder in revulsion.

'What?' Mum was white. 'They did what?' She stood up and moved around the room. I sank further into the chair. I wanted it to swallow me whole, so I didn't have to say anything else. 'Some boys sexually assaulted Annie? You were all drunk? You drink?' She looked at me as if I'd suddenly grown horns out of my head, as if she had never seen me before in her life. 'I'm in shock.'

'I know,' I felt like the adult explaining something elementary to a three-year-old. I watched as my mother's awareness of the world she lived in slipped away. I saw the fear and disorientation on her face as if she suddenly realised she'd ended up in a foreign country and didn't speak the language and had no map. 'There were photos taken.'

'Photos?' Mum sat back in the chair opposite me. 'What do you mean?'

'They photographed her when she was ...' I was going to say passed out again, but I tempered it, 'asleep. And they put them on Facebook.'

'What?' Mum shook her head. 'Why?'

'I don't know — it's just what we do,' I said.

'You do this?' Mum said. 'Did you do this too?' It was as if the pieces slowly joined up in her head. She suddenly realised why I was telling her this unrelated story about a party and Annie. 'What did you do?' And at that point her voice changed. My perplexed mother gave way to fear — and almost anger.

'I did it too,' I said. 'I'm in the photos, I touched Annie too. And now she's in hospital. She tried to kill herself.' The words spewed out of my mouth. 'I'm in serious trouble, Mum.' I wanted her to hold me, comfort me. I wanted her to stroke my hair like she did when I was little and fell over, or lost my bear Binky, but instead she stared at me. She stared at the makeup I wasn't supposed to wear to school. She stared at the top button, which was undone on my uniform. She stared at my rolled-up skirt, my waxed and spray-tanned legs. She stared at the horns growing out of my head. She stared at me as if I was a stranger, and then she put her hands to her face and she cried.

It was a bit of a blur after that. Miss Jones returned with Mr Fletcher. I sat watching them talk to my mother. I listened to them talk. I heard everything, I understood little. I guess it's difficult to comprehend a conversation when the whole time you are trying to fit in the pieces you know are going to bring you down. Everything I knew — and it became apparent I knew so much more than them — was so incriminating. I was the one who was about to undo everyone, myself included.

'Tell us what happened,' Mr Fletcher said to me. He was so stern. So angry. I'd never had much to do with him. I wasn't a captain and I wasn't a troublemaker, so I'd never really had to talk to him before. But now I was a troublemaker of the highest order and suddenly I lost my will to speak. 'This situation is serious, Jasmine. The police accessed Annie's computer last night. They have seen the photos,' he looked disgusted, 'they have spoken to Jack and to Thomas.'

Tommy and Jack. I tried to move my thoughts

along. What had they spoken to them about, in particular? What had Tommy and Jack said? What did the police actually know? Who was I protecting with my silence? 'And they want to speak to you. You're in serious trouble, Jasmine.'

I nodded. I knew I was. I had just needed to hear it. 'What do you want to know?' I asked finally.

'Everything,' he said and nodded to his personal assistant, Mrs Killarney, who picked up a pen and paper.

So I told him everything. Or nearly.

Post 21: Daddy's little girl

I was in Mr Fletcher's office all day. After I made my first confession, several others followed. The police arrived and I had to say it all again, but unlike Mr Fletcher, who let me talk, they kept interrupting me, asking me questions, grilling me over details, time frames, people who were there, who saw what, who sent messages — tiny, minute details of a night I had only a hazy recollection of. Mum sat in the corner and watched the stranger who was once her daughter talk about a life she had no idea ever existed. And every word I spoke pushed her further and further away from me. All I wanted was for my mum to sit next to me and hold my hand, but she wasn't prepared to hold a stranger's hand, to offer words of comfort and support to someone she was just meeting for the very first time.

On the way home the silence in the car was unbearable.

'Does Dad know?' I asked as we pulled into the driveway.

She nodded grimly. 'He's terribly upset by this.'

His car was parked in the garage, he was home. What would he say to me? More importantly, how would he say it? Would he shout? Like he did that time I accidently smashed the Palladian-style window with a rocket ship I'd made. He really lost it then. 'Thousands of dollars, Jasmine!' he'd exploded. Or would he talk to me in that soft voice, which was even worse than jump-scares in a horror movie, never knowing when his soft modulations would give in to raised tones? I felt ill. I walked into the house. I expected to see him at the kitchen table, but he wasn't there. He wasn't in the lounge room. The office door was shut. I knocked tentatively.

'Dad?' I said softly.

There was silence for the longest while. 'Not now, Jasmine,' he said curtly and, like a kicked puppy, I slunk away to my room.

In my room I looked at all the messages I'd missed while I was in Fletcher's office. Mr Fletcher had scowled at me when he heard the ping of my phone. 'Turn it off,' he'd demanded as if it was the most pathetic sound he'd ever heard.

My phone was full of messages. Group text messages from kids at school:

Delete photos

Delete history

Cops involved

Jack and Tommy arrested

Jack and Tommy arrested? The cops hadn't said that. They'd mentioned possession of child pornography and sexual assault. They'd said stuff about investigations and enquiries — they hadn't said arrests. No messages from Jack. Where was he? Was he in prison? I couldn't even imagine it — I didn't know anyone who'd ever gone to prison. What did they do? Hold them in a filthy cell? Was juvenile detention like a prison? I so badly wanted to talk to Jack, but I knew he wouldn't be able to reply.

The cops had told me they'd talk to me again. Mum had asked if charges would be laid against me and the constable had shrugged. 'At this point we are gathering evidence,' was all she'd said. I wondered if I needed a lawyer — I had been in possession of child pornography too. And while my indecent assault of Annie had been 'non-penetrative' it still was classed as a sexual assault. I looked around my room. Everything seemed so unfamiliar. So unforgivable. My parents alienated from me, no discussions, no strategies. I was so very alone.

Now I know what happened that night, I'll give you the facts. When I left the cooking class, this is what happened:

Annie pulled her phone from her pocket and messaged her mum: *Come and get me.* After ten minutes her mum texted back: *Wait until the end of school.* Annie replied: *No* and then switched off her phone. Her mum, sensing something hadn't been right all week, had no choice but to collect her. In the car Annie wouldn't speak, she stared stonily out of the window. She had been betrayed by everyone, me being the last person she ever suspected. She had been horrified when she'd seen what I'd done. At home she went straight to her room and messaged me. But as we all know, I didn't reply. On Facebook she chatted to some people from the party, trying to find out if I was in the room when Jack and Tommy sexually assaulted her. In her mind I was the worst of them all. She believed I was the instigator, that I'd watched and encouraged them, that I'd taken photos and then over the last week I'd pretended to be her friend. No one could give her any satisfactory answers. But this was what she believed. She was betrayed. Abandoned. The last message she sent was to Tommy, who didn't reply, but it said:

You have no idea what it's like to be a girl

Then she went to the bathroom, took a handful of pills and tried to drown herself in the bath.

It's horrific.

But this is what we did.

With our stupid antics. Our stupid drunken antics. Our photos. Our obscene treatment of people. Our fucking sexual assault. We pushed Annie to believe that life wasn't worth living. That she couldn't take it anymore.

Her mum broke the door down. She dragged her from the bath. She breathed into her lungs. She called the ambulance. She tried desperately to save her little girl's life. A life she suddenly realised she knew nothing about. The ambulance came. They got her to hospital. They got her on life support, but they didn't think she'd make it. They warned her family that even if she did, she might be brain-damaged.

This is what we did.

We nearly killed a girl. We shamed her. We assaulted her. We caused unspeakable damage. To her person. To the very essence of who she was.

Post 22: Sorry

Annie, I'm sorry.

I'm so, so sorry.

I have never done anything so terrible in my life. And I hope nothing is ever this terrible again.

I'm sorry for being a part of it.

I'm sorry for treating you that way.

But more than anything I'm sorry for being such a coward.

I'm sorry I wasn't there for you. Because Annie, I believe that if I had been, you wouldn't have done what you did.

And so I'm sorry to your parents. I'm sorry to your sister. I'm sorry for everything that your family has had to endure.

And I wish I could tell you this.

I wish I had the opportunity to tell you.

But I can't.

For that I will always be sorry.

Post 23: What it's like to be a girl

Apologies for my absence, but getting to that part of the story was pretty traumatic for me. It's taken me over a week to get back out of that 'headspace', with more than my usual share of counselling. Remembering how desolate everything was put me in a bit of a funk. But now I'm ready to continue on with what happened next:

I sat in my room and watched Facebook, the kids at school scrambling to delete incriminating messages and pictures. They were so foolish — the police already had Annie's computer. In this time no one posted about Annie. No comments came up about her attempted suicide, or the happenings that had led to it. Where this forum had previously been awash with real and fictional incidents stemming from that night, now there was a collective silence that settled over all things pertaining to Greenheadgate. It was so cowardly. It was so repulsive and I couldn't do anything at all. I was an instigator of the whole terrible affair. I had no voice anymore.

My parents felt the same way about me. Voiceless. Not once that night did either of them come and speak to me. I burned with shame. My self-loathing hit an all-time high. Through my life, despite my looks, I'd suffered the same self-loathing most girls do: too fat, hair boring, boobs too small (yes, that one again), lurking pimple with the proportions of Mount Vesuvius — I'd despised myself plenty of times. But that night it was real. And I knew this was how Annie had felt. She had hated herself so much she couldn't bear to be herself any longer. She had taken the abuse, the insults, the betrayal, the shame, so far into herself that she couldn't find her way out. She had tried to just not be anymore. I shuddered. I contemplated: did I hate myself that much? Could I also do that? My parents had rejected me. My friends had blanked me. I had probably ruined my future. Those pictures, the police said, were irretrievable and could resurface years later when I wanted to apply for a job, when I wanted to get married. The constable had said in her cold voice, 'They will never leave you alone. When you don't suspect it, they will reappear and you'll be facing this judgement again.'

I would face this judgement for the rest of my life. Could I handle it? I must admit there were several moments that night where I thought I couldn't. Where I thought I should do what Annie did. But where she'd failed I'd succeed, because in my misery I knew neither of my parents would be banging down my door. If I actually attempted what Annie had, I'd see it through to the end. No one would save me. I can't tell you how much I cried that night. But by about one thirty in the morning I knew I had only one choice. There was only one option available to me and that was to save myself. Annie was right when she said to Tommy, 'You have no idea what it's like to be a girl.'

But I did.

Post 24: Saving Jazz

I will condense what happened over the next few months, for the sake of brevity, and give you what I believe are the pertinent facts to the next stage of the saga. Bear with me, dear reader, and should the need arise, comment on the bottom of the post if you feel I've failed to explain anything — I'll address only reasonable comments. Oh, and by the way, Lani Gray, you have been blocked from posting comments. You are a typical example of how hatred is spread in this world and this blog is about making amends, not providing you with another forum to perpetuate your petty-minded thoughts (if a single-cell amoeba is capable of having thoughts, I know that's hate in itself, hypocrisy right — so what, it's my blog).

I never returned to school after that day in Mr

Fletcher's office. I've been studying Distance Ed, but that is trivial and I can go into it later. I wasn't expelled — or excluded, or whatever the term is — but my parents made a decision to keep me home. It wasn't like they wanted me around them, but maybe it was more like a bit of parental protection — a part of me hoped so. The town had gone wild.

Jack and Tommy had also been kept home by their parents. They were facing a range of sex charges. By all accounts they were both being cooperative and both had admitted their guilt, but this was where the rift occurred in Greenhead. Two camps sprang up. The first camp saw Tommy and Jack as criminals in their own right, but also as the embodiment of a generation gone crazy, a generation seeking approval through social media, engaging in lewd and illegal activities, creators and consumers of pornography. This camp, led by the likes of Mr Maitland (who'd tell anyone who cared to listen that he'd identified this trait in Jack as a ten-year-old boy — 'If you can easily kill a fish then this is to be expected'), wanted the book thrown at them (which highlighted the generational differences — more likely throw an iPad at them). The other camp was marked by the war cry 'They're just boys'. Those in this camp were incensed by the criminal charges against 'kids having fun', 'a prank', 'boys being boys'.

The effect was a major schism down the town's centre, the bristling animosity of a town divided. People closed ranks, became secretive and suspicious of one another. As for me, Jazz Lovely — at this point I wasn't even on the town radar.

My father didn't actually speak to me until two days after the principal's office. He purposefully avoided me. If I heard him moving around in the kitchen, when I walked in I'd see the swinging door he'd exited through. Mum and Dad weren't sitting me down for concerned parental chats, they weren't offering me support and unconditional love. In fact, I think it's fair to say in those first weeks they had stopped loving me and when all the details emerged (yes, there are more revelations to come) Dad retreated further from me. His revulsion for me was palpable; he couldn't bear to be in the same room with me. My fear of how he'd speak to me was totally unfounded. He actually had no intention of speaking to me at all. Mum was a bit more involved.

She would speak to me, even make eye contact for as long as she could, then glance away blinking madly, as if a bug or something had flown into her eye. Before the trials started I moved to my Aunty Jane's in Perth. It made sense anyway — that way I could get to court easily and they wouldn't have to look at the subject of their shame daily.

But I'm jumping ahead. I was a prisoner in my room, tethered to my laptop and phone as my only connections to the real world, yet too frightened to communicate through them. I couldn't comment or message anyone. I just watched the world on Facebook. Isolated and alone.

Then Dad knocked on my door. 'Jasmine.' The sound of his voice made me want to cry. My heart leapt and I actually started trembling. He had come to talk to me.

'Yes,' I jumped from my bed and faced the door. I'd never been particularly close to my dad, he wasn't really hands-on. He was really just a constant figure in my life, but over the last two days I had missed him so much. Missed his approval of me. He opened the door and his frame filled the doorway.

'The police are here,' he spoke coldly to my

Chinese waving-cat on the window ledge. 'They want to speak to you.' Then he turned around and walked away. I felt like vomiting. Dad wasn't going to support me — I heard the office door shut. He was going to leave me to face the cops on my own. At that moment, despite everything I'd done, I actually hated my father.

Mum was in the lounge room with the two police officers when I entered. She was seated, they were standing. The female cop had a notebook in her hands.

'We have a few questions to ask you,' the policeman said. I nodded. 'We have had Thomas and Jack assisting in our enquiries but there is something neither of them can answer. There is a disparity in the photographs that circulated after the incident.' He held two photographs in front of me. I took them and placed them on the table. It was like those puzzles in the paper — *Can you find ten differences?* The two images were both of Annie lying on the bed. In one she was fully dressed, permanent marker visible on parts of her body (clearly taken after all the abuse), the blanket bunched over her feet (not over her, as I had left it — was this

Callum's photo?). In the other she was naked and there was no blanket, the permanent marker clearly visible all over her body. I blinked back tears as I looked again at the images. I kept staring at both photographs, feeling like I had found about nine differences — where was the tenth?

'Here,' the cop said, circling some of the writing on her naked body, 'and then here,' he circled the corresponding area on the dressed one. Bingo! The tenth difference — so obvious, so apparent. 'Who did that?' he asked.

I looked at the images. **JACK WAS HERE** and an arrow, then the other one: ██████ **WAS HERE** and an arrow. I felt cold. I looked at my mother, who looked away, rubbing at the insect in her eye. 'Me,' I said pathetically.

It was enough for them to take me to the police station for further questioning. They advised my mum to get me a lawyer and said there was no doubt I was going to face charges. They listed indecent assault, concealing a crime, conspiracy. That day was terrifying, in so many ways. The crimes were not going to go unpunished. We would pay for what we'd done.

Post 25: The crimes

I was never detained by the police. I was questioned, at length. They were trying to see what part I had played in the sexual assault on Annie, whether I had been there during it, if I had contributed to it and why I had covered up for Jack. They believed me when I said I hadn't known about the assault when I erased Jack's name, that I had unintentionally covered up his crime (if not for all the visual footage). For my part I would face the judge in the Children's Court and my lawyer advised me I wouldn't be incarcerated.

'Community service, possible fine, bit of a slap on the wrist,' he said comfortingly. At that stage he was pretty much the only comfort I got. Dad had zero tolerance for me and Mum was merely a physical presence, to take me to the cops or my lawyer. She was probably more relieved than anyone when I moved to Aunty Jane's.

I couldn't stand living in a tomb, with two people who clearly hated me, in a town of people who all hated me. When my involvement became known around town — after Mrs Weaver next door saw the cops escort me from my house — no one was divided over my actions, as they had been about Tommy and Jack. I wasn't considered a prankster or 'just being a girl'. No, I was considered abnormal, base, depraved — what kind of girl would do that to her best friend? I was seen as a freak — a scourge. If it had been Plymouth or Salem in the 1600s they would have branded a gigantic red A (not for adultery, but assault) across my chest. I was a social pariah.

I had to get out, and suicide was not going to be an option. Aunty Jane knew the sugar-coated details from Mum, so when I rang her in desperation asking if I could stay for a bit her reply was, 'As long as you need,' and within a couple of hours she picked me up.

I sat in the front seat of her battered VW van as

she drove too fast from Greenhead. I didn't feel any sorrow leaving the town behind. In fact, as I watched it disappear in the side mirror a lot of the tension and stress fell away. I wasn't out of it yet, but at least I was out of there.

Aunty Jane was always a bit of a hippy, burning foul incense and doing yoga. She was married to my dad's brother, but the polar opposite of Mum, who was so fucking uptight and stymied by appearances. I think that was the worst part of it for Mum — what the neighbours thought. Like who'd give a shit about Mrs Weaver's opinion anyway — the woman thought her bespoke bronze nude statue, urinating into her pond, was the height of class.

Aunty Jane and my Uncle Rob were a lot younger than my mum and dad, who had always seemed much older than everyone else's parents anyway. There were about twelve years between Dad and Rob, his brother, and Rob had always lived in Australia, whereas Dad had grown up in Johannesburg. When I'd look at Rob I'd see the family resemblance, but even his posture was relaxed and chilled. I guess Aunty Jane just had that effect on everyone. She ran an online homemade craft business, everything from macrame pot holders ('I'm bringing back all things retro,' she'd say with a piece of twine between her teeth as she fashioned a new design) to homemade kasundi. She was even trialling a range of teas (because 'a lot of the tea franchises are ethically corrupt'). She glanced over at me as we neared Joondalup. She had slowed from a hundred and thirty to about ninety, only twenty over the speed limit.

'How are you travelling?' she asked finally.

I shrugged. 'Okay. I can't thank you enough for rescuing me.' As I spoke the words thickened. I was teetering close to the edge and Aunty Jane was the first person to show me an inch of compassion.

'Not a drama, kid,' she said and even her voice, so soft and Australian, seemed gentler than my mother's clipped words. 'Do you want to fill me in?'

I nodded. 'I'll tell you everything, but I'm afraid you are going to hate me when you hear the real details instead of my mother's sanitised version.' I was trying not to panic, but what if Aunty Jane didn't like what she heard, turned the car around and took me back there? I wouldn't survive in that town. To my horror, she swerved off the road and banged the

VW up over the kerb, onto the nature strip.

She turned to face me. 'Okay. These are the rules. It's about honesty and trust. From what I've been told, you fucked up. But what you don't know is that we all fuck up, to varying degrees, at some stage. I'm here because you need me. And I'll do what I can to help you through this and get over it. That's what you need to know.'

'Why?' I asked through tears. Why would my aunt, who was only related to me by marriage, offer me the things my parents wouldn't?

'Because that's what family does,' Aunty Jane said. 'Relax.' She pulled her sleeve up and showed me her tattoo — *breathe*. 'I have it here to remind me, all the time, to slow down and just breathe. Okay?'

I nodded and inhaled deeply. 'Okay. This is what happened ...' And I was still talking when we pulled up in front of her house right on the edge of Perth city.

The house was an old federation style — dark-red brick, white window trims and worn weathered floorboards. Aunty Jane opened the front door to a sight that was worlds away from my mother's pristine place. 'This is why we have Christmas at your folks'," she said, kicking a kid's toy out the way. 'I don't think Meghan can handle the clutter.'

Clutter was polite. The house looked like a tornado of eight-year-olds had swept through and dropped every toy currently in stock at Kmart on the floor. In the kitchen the dishes were piled high. 'Dishwasher broke down and today is ...' Aunty Jane looked at the roster on the fridge, 'Louie's turn. Hang on a sec. Louie?' she bellowed down another hallway. Within minutes my twelve-year-old cousin Louie — one half of the monozygotes, the other being Charlie — emerged scratching his belly.

'Wassup mum?' he asked. Despite the fact it was after lunch, it was clear Louie had just woken up. He saw me. 'Hey Jazzy, wassup?'

'Hey Louie,' I gave him a wooden hug. Never having had a sibling, I found myself supremely awkward.

'Dishes,' Aunty Jane said, nodding to the kitchen sink. Louie nodded and loped over. 'Jazz is coming to stay with us for a while.'

'Cool,' Louie said and started washing up.

'Come on, I'll show you your room.' Aunty Jane led me through the house and out into the back garden. It was a big block — not by Greenhead standards, but in the inner city it was the kind of place people bought, bulldozed and subdivided into three or more townhouses. 'I won't hear of demolition talk,' Aunty Jane told me, 'it's a crime to knock down these old places. A part of our Australian history. And that tree,' she pointed to an enormous gum tree, 'is about two hundred years old. It's a piece of living history.' I'd been to Aunty Jane's a handful of times in my life. It was true that family gatherings were always at my parents' place, no doubt because Mum's nerves couldn't handle the ramshackle approach to domestic duties at Aunty Jane's. But I never remembered the little timber cabin that sat nestled in the back corner of the garden.

'Is that new?' I asked pointing to it. It was the cutest thing I'd ever seen. It was bright blue with white wooden French windows and doors, a verandah and a wide timber deck.

'Yes,' Aunty Jane nodded and produced a key. 'It was finished last week. Fortuitous, really, because I wouldn't want you having to share with Bernie — or heaven forbid Bernie and Jake having to share.'

Bernie and Jake were the two younger twins, nine years old. Aunty Jane said she had a knack for producing duplicate children. 'A backup plan, if the first one goes rotten,' she said with a laugh. A house full of boys. I wondered what it would be like. The inside of the cabin had polished timber floors, a double bed, a wardrobe, dresser and an air con. It was pretty and tidy. 'Once you're settled we can get stuff to personalise it — make it yours.'

I sat on the bed. 'Thank you so much,' I said. She waved my gratitude away.

'Did you build this as a guest room?' I asked.

'Amongst other things.' Aunty Jane wheeled my suitcase to the wardrobe.

'Was this going to be your workroom?' I asked as it suddenly occurred to me.

'Yes,' Aunty Jane put her hand up to stop my protestations. 'Don't even,' she warned me. 'This is a perfect space for you. You can't live in the house surrounded by the brat pack. You're a girl. You need space. You need privacy.'

'But your work?' I felt guilty. She had built this to create her pot hangers and tea trials. She hadn't even got to use it before she gave it to me.

'Honey, I've run my business out of the back room for this long. I'm so used to it. Don't. Promise me you'll let me do this for you. Don't take away the thrill I get out of giving you this room. That would be rude.'

I snapped my mouth shut and nodded.

'Now have a shower — I even got this thing plumbed. Through there,' she pointed to a timber panelled door that blended in perfectly with the wall. 'It's little, but it has a shower, basin and loo.'

'Thank you so much,' I said meekly.

'And enough of that too. Get sorted and we'll talk later.'

I didn't know whether to kiss her — that wasn't part of my family's repertoire — but I had to hug her.

'One last time,' I said, hugging her. 'Thank you.'

'One last time,' she agreed, returning my hug.

Aunty Jane provided me with a sanctuary, but more importantly she gave me support and love. I know I would have made it — but if it hadn't been for her, I'm not sure how.

Post 26: A new day

The night I arrived, after the boys were in bed, we had a council of war meeting in the lounge room. Aunty Jane and Uncle Rob shared a bottle of red. I drank tea — one of Aunty Jane's relaxing brews. We discussed my options.

'First, school,' Uncle Rob said. He pushed his hair back with one hand, a gesture I learnt was his trademark. 'What do you want to do?'

I shook my head. I never got to make decisions with my parents — I was always told where I was going, what I was doing, what I should look like, what my future would be. 'I don't know,' I said. The idea of going back into a school environment filled me with dread.

'I don't think a standard school is suitable right

now,' Uncle Rob said, as if reading my mind. 'You've got all the other stuff to deal with and I think the last thing you need is being around kids who are following the action.' He was right. I knew that when the video went viral, kids in the city had commented on it. If I attended a normal school I'd be *that* girl — the one who did *those* things. I'd never be free of it.

'Distance Ed,' Aunty Jane said. She looked at Rob, who nodded in agreement.

'Great idea, babe,' he said, 'you're not just a pretty face.'

'That's why he married me,' Aunty Jane tapped her head, 'up here for thinking, down there for dancing. Do you know intelligence is inherited on the X chromosome? So all boys get their intelligence from their mothers.'

'I got lucky,' Rob said, 'the boys will be clever like their mother and not as dumb as me.'

'You're not *that* dumb,' Aunty Jane said. They shared a smile and I watched in wonder. I had never seen my parents engage with each other like that. There was always aloofness between them. I could almost imagine them referring to each other as Mr Lovely and Mrs Lovely in conversation. Until now, I'd never realised how Jane Austen my parents had been.

'Distance Ed,' I mulled this idea over. It would mean I'd get to stay here, holed up in this sanctuary — away from the hate of the wider community. No idea had ever felt so appealing in my life.

'I'll make some calls tomorrow,' Aunty Jane said. 'As for tomorrow, we've got a few things to do. You need to learn the public transport system — so you're not a prisoner in this house.'

'I don't mind being a prisoner,' I said.

'Yes, well, I still want you to be a teenager — you still need to get out and about.'

Later in bed I thought over the last twenty-four hours. So much had happened, and for the first time in ages it had been positive. I felt a glimmer of hope — I might actually get through this ordeal. But as for getting out and about, where would I go, and who with?

In the morning I awoke disoriented. I sat up in bed and gazed around as I slowly remembered where I was. I stepped out and walked to the main house. The back door was open, but the house was empty and the kitchen looked like every dish and piece of cutlery had been used. There were crumbs over the bench, on the floor, even on the dog. I was wiping the last plate up when Aunty Jane walked in the front door.

'Morning,' she said offering me a takeaway coffee. She looked at the kitchen in astonishment. 'Granite benchtops!' she exclaimed loudly. 'Who'd have thought under all that crap there was granite!'

I laughed and hung the tea towel on the hook.

'Seriously, Jazz, you're not here as the hired help. We have a roster in place. It's community work.'

'I have to be allowed to help,' I held my hands up at her protestations. 'Otherwise I won't feel like I really belong here.' And already, so quickly, there was nowhere else in the world that I wanted to belong more than here, in this house, with these crazy and alive people. It was so much better than living in a mausoleum. 'And besides,' I said stealing her line, 'you wouldn't want to take away the thrill I get out of doing this for you. It would be rude.'

Aunty Jane laughed, a really loud laugh. 'Jazz, that isn't going to be a problem. You already belong with us.'

Post 27: New beginnings

The first week at Aunty Jane's was full of new beginnings. Aunty Jane certainly didn't waste any time in getting me settled into the city. Firstly, she got me a referral to a psychologist.

'You need this for so many reasons,' she explained, driving me to the psych's office. 'Also, in order to be eligible for Distance Ed we need a psych to agree to the special circumstances.'

'But what about the cost?' I asked. So far I'd been at Aunty Jane's for a week and the cost of living had never been raised. I needed to know that I could contribute to the living expenses, and as far as I was concerned washing dishes and running a vacuum over the floor wasn't enough. Aunty Jane watched me out of the corner of her eye.

'Your mum's been in touch,' she said softly.

'Mum?' I was surprised. Since we'd broken the land speed record escaping Greenhead (and I always thought of that drive as an escape) neither one of my parents had been in touch with me. At first I'd expected a text, or a call, but as the days passed I realised they were just as relieved as me about our parting ways. It still hurt. 'What did she say?'

'She wanted to know how you were,' Aunty Jane eased the car into the psychologist's car park and turned the engine off. 'Believe me, I was going to tell you — I just wanted to make sure you were settled in first.' I was feeling totally nauseous. Was I expected to take this as a token of my mother's interest in me? It couldn't be further from the truth — it was a clear, neon signal of her disregard for me. 'I told her you were doing alright, that we were working out school and things. That the kids love you and so do me and Rob.'

'And?' I knew there was more, 'what did she really want?'

Aunty Jane shook her head, 'She wanted to let me know that she and your father wanted to provide an allowance to you and expenses to me and Rob.'

I nodded. Of course. Keep everything business-like. Don't burden anyone, and if you have to, then make sure you pay for it. That was their way. 'Are they giving you enough?' I asked bitterly.

'Hey,' Aunty Jane put a hand on my arm, 'I don't want their money.'

'No, I'm sorry,' I put my hand on hers in horror. 'I'm not upset with you and Uncle Rob. They *should* give you money. And it better be enough. It's just,' I shrugged helplessly, 'that's all they can do for me, you know? They can't love me, so they just pay for me.' Tears rose again. Every time I thought of them in their cold mortuary I wanted to weep.

'I know, honey,' Aunty Jane squeezed my hand, 'I know it seems like they don't love you, but they really do. They just have a funny way of showing it.'

'Well,' I wiped my eyes with the back of my hand, 'I guess the psych is really going to believe I qualify for Distance Ed now, hey?' I laughed, even if it did sound forced.

The psych was a small dark-haired woman named Karan. She had the paperwork filled in and submitted to Distance Ed ready for Term Two. She also had me booked for weekly appointments so we could work through my many issues, particularly those regarding my parents and my upcoming criminal trial. Karan was non-judgemental. She explained to me a lot of things about my behaviour and the need we had for approval and a sense of belonging. By the end of the term (I had been off school nearly eight weeks and at Aunty Jane's for most of it) I felt confident that I would be able to study and complete Year 10.

I also got a job. At the end of Aunty Jane's street was a coffee strip, very trendy and very busy. Aunty Jane and I would take turns each morning to fetch the coffee, which we would invariably drink in the backyard, chatting about the headlines in the daily paper (collecting the paper was the coffee-getter's responsibility). This must've been the first time in my life I ever had meaningful conversations with an adult. In fact, with anyone. I was slowly starting to realise how insular my Greenhead existence had been. But anyway, I digress. Aunty Jane and I constantly argued over who made the best coffee. She said Chicco, I said Skinny Cow. Day after day this light banter continued until I decided I would win the debate once and for all — even if it meant stooping to low levels of trickery and deceit. This was my plan: get two takeaway cups from Skinny Cow, go to Chicco and buy two coffees, transfer them into my favourite shop's cups and present them to Aunty Jane. She'll proceed to screw up her nose, huff and sigh as she drinks her (favourite) coffee and tell me how like wet cardboard it tastes and how that shop should be shut by the Health Department pronto (or something in this vein). When I reveal that it's actually Chicco's coffee she has just bagged out, she'll have to admit that Skinny Cow is superior.

And this is what happened: after procuring my cups from Skinny Cow, I go behind enemy lines for the first time: Chicco. I notice the barista the moment I walk through the door. He is medium height, strong build (I see his biceps through his tight shirt), dark Italian complexion and I place him at about eighteen. His face is perfection, he has to be the hottest guy — in real life — that I've ever seen. Think Channing Tatum and you'll get close. He smiles at me and asks what I'd like.

'Two skinny lattes,' I say, and as I rifle through my bag for my purse I absentmindedly take out the opposition's cups and put them on the counter.

'Oh no!' I look up at his loud exclamation. He has picked the cups up and is staring at them in horror. 'What is this? My beautiful girl — you're seeing another barista?' He is feigning hurt indignation — I know it's an act, but it's drawing attention my way, the last thing I want in the world. 'What has happened between us, bella? I thought we were so tight.'

'Sorry,' I gather the cups up and tuck them in my bag, mortified. 'It's a trick on my aunt, you see,' and I try to explain my clever plan, which now sounds decidedly stupid.

'Your aunt?' he looks at me with his soulful brown eyes. 'Is she as beautiful as you?'

'No,' I say, and then wave my hands in the air. I'm going from mortified to horrified. 'I don't mean she's not as beautiful as me, she is. Not that I'm saying I'm beautiful. I'm not. Not beautiful, that is. I mean,' I keep waving my hands stupidly, 'anyway, she's not really my aunt.'

'So who is she, this not-aunt of yours?' he asks quizzically.

'Jane Lovely,' I say shaking my head, wishing he'd

make the coffee so I could get the hell out of there and never come back. No matter what Aunty Jane thought of their coffee, I was never setting foot in this shop ever again. 'She is my aunt, but by marriage I mean.'

'Oh, Miss Jane Lovely,' he beams at me, 'She *is* lovely. The loveliest woman in the world.' He sighs softly. 'That is, until I met you. What's your name?'

'Jazz,' I mutter.

'Ah, beautiful music, musical Jazz, she drinks shiraz,' he starts singing this made-up song as he finally makes the coffee. 'I'm Frank,' he smiles. 'Cups?' he demands of me.

'Pardon?' I just want to pay and go. Or just go.

'The cups from the *Cow*,' he spits the word out. 'I'll play this trick with you, see. And when you know my coffee is better than theirs you'll come and work with me. I'll give you a job as a barista and then you'll marry me.'

I shake my head at him. He may be hot but he's several coffee beans short of an espresso. 'Sure.' I hand him the cups and he tips the coffee in them.

'So it's a deal? If she says this coffee, Chicco's, is better than Skinny Cow's — despite this elaborate hoax — you'll agree to work for me. Marriage, we can discuss later.'

'Sure,' I repeat. At that point I'd agree to anything just to get out of there.

'Promise?' he says, taking my hand to shake.

'I promise,' I agree, returning his strong grip.

'See you soon, my little Shiraz,' Frank calls after me.

I watched Aunty Jane over the rim of my cardboard cup. I wanted to tell her about Crazy Frank, but that would have blown my trick, so I waited. She sipped the coffee and frowned. She raised an eyebrow and looked at me, then sipped again. I could barely stand the tension.

'Well then,' she said finally.

'Well then, what?' I asked.

'I don't like being wrong,' she said, 'Rob will attest to that. But, honey, I've got to admit, this tastes as good as Chicco coffee. If I didn't know better I'd have to say it was of a higher quality. There is a hint of vanilla in this that I've never tasted before, not even in Chicco coffee. So I guess that's it. You're right. Skinny Cow is the best latte on the strip.'

I looked at her in horror. That wasn't meant to happen. 'Oh,' I said.

'Oh?' Aunty Jane smiled, 'in this house it's okay to gloat. You were right. This is the best coffee. I'm converted. I'm never going back into Chicco, despite the cute barista.'

'Frank,' I said.

Aunty Jane nodded and then frowned. 'Yes, Frank — how do you know him?'

I told her of my trick, I told her about Frank and the job offer and proposal. She laughed hysterically. 'Oh Jazz, this is absolutely priceless! So I am right about the coffee! And you've got yourself a job. Winner, winner, chicken dinner.'

'Yes, but I'm not going back there,' I stated firmly.

'Oh yes you are,' Aunty Jane said nodding, 'let's call it your punishment for trying to deceive your frail old aunt.'

'Seriously?'

'Seriously.'

The next day I ventured back into Chicco. If I was going to change who I had been, that meant taking chances, and making different, better decisions. If Aunty Jane thought this was a good thing for me — 'You get to meet people who know nothing about you, who see you as that beautiful girl from the coffee shop' — then I had to believe it was.

'My Shiraz,' Frank signalled me as I walked in the doorway. 'Come to start work?'

I nodded, he beamed. 'Excellent, tie this on and let me show you how we can make magic together.' I took the apron and tied it around my waist, pulled my hair back and rolled up my sleeves.

Post 28: The forgotten

Time kept us all moving forward. Me, Tommy and
Jack towards our judgement, and Annie towards her
death. She had been on life support for about three
months when the decision was made to turn it off.
At the risk of the haters twisting this around (don't
worry, I know pretty much who you are), several
things ran through my mind: Why? Would turning
it off mean she would die? If she died, how would
that impact upon our court cases next week? Forgive
me, dear reader, if this is all too callous for you — it
sounds a lot more callous than it really was. I was
terrified of Annie's death. I desperately didn't want
her to die, because I didn't want her death on my
conscience — it's true. But it was much more than
that. I didn't want her not to be anymore. I loved the

world that had Annie in it, and though I knew there would be no place for Jazz Lovely in her life if she survived, I didn't care. I wanted there to be a world in which Annie lived, met people, fell in love, could be the Annie she wanted to be. And I knew Death was not that place.

But they were going to switch life support off.

This I learnt through Facebook. It would be hard for anyone over thirty to understand what it meant to a fifteen-year-old to watch the world go by and have no voice in it. But that was my exile. While I awaited judgement I had to retain 'full radio silence' — and so I did, but it didn't mean I couldn't be a silent spectator. Which I was. The updates arrived daily about switching Annie off. Annie — the ho, slut, whore, the one who got what she asked for — was suddenly the poster girl for the whole generation. Her greatest haters became her fiercest supporters — 'Save Our Annie!'. It was truly sickening. But of course no one knew why they were pulling the plug. The Townshends had no public profile. Information was trickled through family and friends, so no one went to any lengths to explain why they were doing it. Any comment about 'pulling the plug' on Annie was countered with sympathy and condolences and hang-in-there icons. The whole thing made me sick to my stomach.

Post 29: Judgement

I had my day in court. Aunty Jane and Uncle Rob
drove me.

'We'll be there the whole time,' Aunty Jane said
on the way, squeezing my hand. As I faced the judge
and the charges were read, in that moment when
I had reached the lowest point of my relatively
shallow existence, I looked across to see Aunty Jane
and Uncle Rob sitting there smiling supportively at
me, and next to them was my mum, and next to her
was my dad.

Will Sanderson defended me strongly. He
played up my strengths, he expressed my remorse,
he elucidated carefully my pristine track record.
He appealed to the judge for her greatest leniency.
And might I tell you, dear reader, at this point I

wasn't worried about my sentence, whether I'd be incarcerated, how much community service or whatever punishment was to be meted out to me. All I could think was *At least I have a chance*. At least this isn't it for me. They were pulling the plug on Annie and I was receiving my judgement — but I knew mine wasn't final.

I stood nervously before the judge. Though I had always hated the judgement of others, this was unavoidable. This was, in a sense, right. I had done something terrible and I was to be judged for those actions.

She looked at me and a small smile played across her lips. 'Jasmine Lovely, you have pleaded guilty to the charge of indecent assault and so I have no other recourse but to impose a sentence against you.

'Before I do, I would like to acknowledge the qualities and attributes expressed by Mr Sanderson, that until now you had never found yourself in court, nor even the principal's office. To say these actions were the result of a lapse of reason, caused by excessive consumption of alcohol, would be fair. I understand that the world you live in is a fast and evolving one, bolstered by the ever-increasing technology at your fingertips. It makes for an exciting and brave new world, doesn't it?' the judge paused to smile again.

'With every brave new world we face brave new challenges. Among them is learning to adjust a teenage mentality and capability to the access of images hitherto not readily accessible.

'I understand that your generation is, on the surface, far more experienced and worldly than previous generations. As digital natives, born with a mobile phone in one hand and a mouse in the other, your generation has never known a world where technology like this didn't exist. This is the culture you have inherited by birthright.

'But, it would be fair to add, your generation is only seemingly worldly. Young and impressionable minds are exposed incessantly to sexualised images of women and, increasingly, to pornography. This creates a false reality, where young girls believe this is how women act. And, at the risk of widening the generation gap further, it saddens me.

'There is nothing to be done to halt this technological revolution; there is only, as always, education. Unfortunately for you, Miss Lovely, your education has come at a great cost. I am imposing ten hours of community service, to be served at a women's shelter. As you are fifteen years old, and provided there are no further charges or convictions against your name, you can be assured this will be erased from your record when you reach eighteen years.' The judge stood and left the room.

I stood next to Will, shaking and trembling with relief, fear, humiliation. I was in a whirl of emotions. Ten hours with women who had been victims of sexual abuse and violence. I saw the judge's reasoning, but the idea was frightening.

Facing my parents after the sentence was handed down was almost as terrifying as facing the judge. Aunty Jane hugged me tightly. 'It'll be alright,' she whispered in my hair, and I wasn't sure if she meant my punishment or seeing my parents.

I looked at my mother and made towards her. She opened her arms and I stepped into them woodenly. She gave me her stiff hug. When I pulled back her face looked a little uncomposed. My father nodded at me and then dropped his eyes. I didn't venture towards him — his body language was clear.

In the restaurant we sat in awkward silence while Aunty Jane filled the conversation with what the two sets of twins were doing, and how I was going with my study and work. Uncle Rob dropped in a few comments, but for the most part he watched his brother studiously ignore me.

'You have a job at a coffee shop?' my mother asked, her nose wrinkling slightly.

'Yes,' I murmured, 'I work Saturdays and Sundays and I'm saving my money for ... well I'm not sure yet, something.' I couldn't look either one of them in the eyes. It was easy with Dad, as his gaze never fell on me, but every now and again Mum's would.

'That's good,' Mum said, although it sounded like she thought it was a terrible idea. 'We've sold the winery,' she added finally.

'For serious?' I exclaimed. I'd had no idea. 'Why?'

'Why?' My dad's voice jolted me and I stared at him. His blue eyes were cold as they finally met with mine. 'Because you made it impossible for us to stay there, Jasmine. The public ridicule of Greenhead. The things people think about your mother and me, the way we raised you to act in such a depraved and perverted way.' His hatred of me was palpable. 'We couldn't live there. We're moving to South Australia. We've bought a winery in the Barossa Valley. We leave in two months. A new beginning.'

A new beginning that didn't include me. I was mortally wounded. My father hated his only child enough to leave her and move to another city, where people wouldn't know of his shame and embarrassment. And as for my mother — was she so weak and pathetic, so totally dependent on him, that she'd do whatever he said? They made me sick to my core.

'Of course,' I almost whispered, using the pre-Greenheadgate voice I'd always reserved for discussions with my parents. I found myself sliding back into that Jasmine. The one who tried to be quiet and good and go unnoticed.

'Hey, that's a little harsh, Paul,' Aunty Jane said angrily.

Uncle Rob levelled my father. 'When are you going to be the parent and accept your kid made a mistake that she's sorry for? When are you going to stop bullying her? Because if you apply your usual hard and cold logic to this, Paul, bullying is what got her in this position.' He crossed his arms.

'Rob, I don't need any advice from a tree-hugging, left-wing do-gooder on how to raise a child,' Dad snapped. 'Nor do I need a lecture on what constitutes bullying. In this instance it is Jasmine, and not me, who committed the crimes.'

'No, you're right,' Uncle Rob stood and held his hands up in surrender, 'let's just pretend none of this is happening, surely that'll fix it? As for crimes, jeez, seriously, Paul — the kid made a mistake. She's no criminal.'

'That's not what the legal system believes,' Dad said righteously. Rob sighed, defeated by Dad's black-and-white approach to life.

Aunty Jane rose, signalling for me to leave with them. 'I'm grateful for this, believe me, otherwise I'd never have got the daughter I always longed for. So for that and your uptight ways I thank you from the bottom of my heart.'

Mum rose as I did. I didn't know what to do. My fiercely loyal aunty and uncle were waiting for me, and my mother teetered between whatever maternal feelings she had and my overbearing father. I looked at Aunty Jane and Uncle Rob and I knew they'd want me to do whatever I felt was right.

'Bye, Mum,' I said, kissing her cheek lightly. And then I grabbed hold of my aunty's hand, the woman who wanted to be my mother, the one who had just claimed me as her daughter, and I actually felt okay as I walked away with them.

'I'm sorry,' Aunty Jane said as we got in the car. She had tears in her eyes.

'What for?' I asked. I was in turmoil. Feelings of abandonment and relief rushed through me, alternating, everything being tempered by these people who had stood up for me. Who were truly the loveliest people in the world. Aunty Jane, who had married a name, but really owned it properly.

'Speaking to your father like that,' Aunty Jane said. 'Truthfully I've never gotten on with him. So different to my Rob. Often I wondered if Rob would one day turn out to be like Paul. I lived in fear — until I realised that Rob was a world and a culture away from his brother. That siblings don't necessarily behave the same way. But that aside, he is your father and I'm sorry.'

'I'm not,' Uncle Rob said. 'He should have been told a few truths a long time ago.'

I still couldn't believe anyone had spoken to my father like that. Dr Paul Lovely. He would be horrified. 'It's okay. He's made it clear what he wants in this world. And I know it would be harder if I didn't have you and Uncle Rob, but I do. So I'm okay.'

'I know you are,' Aunty Jane said. 'You are doing better than okay.'

Post 30: Punishment

After the court hearing everything hit me big-time
and I could feel myself sliding into a dark funk.
I hated myself so much it was a struggle to get out
of bed. I'd do my classes in the morning and my
homework in the evening. I had no social life and
no real contact from anyone in Greenhead. Initially
Sim and Lily and the girls had sent messages, but
when I failed to reply they'd given up. I saw photos
on Facebook from the river cruise. I had been so
looking forward to it — it was a huge night for our
year group. Scrolling through them made me feel so
nostalgic and even homesick — though I knew there
was no home there for me anymore.

I still couldn't find out any details on Annie.
Her death hung over me. Karan increased our

appointments, as I was having such a hard time coming to terms with what we'd done. I know I was found guilty of indecent assault, but to my mind that was a question of semantics. According to the Sexual Assault Resource Centre rape is any unwanted sexual act or behaviour which a person did not consent to — and that was what we had done. Tommy was a rapist. Jack was a rapist. And I couldn't deny it to myself — I was a rapist, too.

'Hey,' Aunty Jane called through the window, 'what you up to?'

'Studying,' I called as she walked into my cabin.

'On Facebook?' she laughed as she sat on my bed.

'Yeah,' I twisted my hair wistfully, 'sometimes I just watch, to see what's going on. Still can't find out anything about Annie.' I shrugged and wiped the tears away. 'Oh Aunty Jane, I feel so terrible.'

'I know, honey,' she put an arm around me.

'I mean, I wouldn't go to her funeral — I wouldn't be welcome and I couldn't face those people. It's just … I need to know.'

'I'll make a call,' Aunty Jane pulled her phone out of her pocket.

'Who?' I asked, alarmed. 'Who will you call?'

'Your mother,' Aunty Jane said, walking out on to the deck.

I tried not to listen, but I couldn't help it. Aunty Jane's voice was low, and she was making a lot of single-word responses. 'Right. Yes. Thanks. I'll tell her.' She came in and gave me a small smile. My stomach was dipping and rolling.

'Annie's not dead,' she said.

'What?' I wiped the tears away. 'Why did they say that then? All that shit on Facebook. What was that all about?'

'They did turn the machine off, honey,' Aunty Jane said, 'but they knew she was going to be able to breathe on her own. She was progressing — so she is home now, but the family, like a few others, have put their house up for sale. They haven't returned there, and your mother doesn't know where they're living now. I think Greenhead is becoming a bit of a ghost town.'

'I don't understand. If she's alive, is she okay?'

'I'm not sure. Your mum seemed to think she was still having a lot of rehabilitation. No one really knows. The Townshends are pretty private people.

Shall we go for a walk?'

I nodded and pulled my Skechers on. We walked down the road. The sun was setting, the Geraldton wax bushes were in full bloom and their purple flowers made everything feel slightly surreal. It was like my two worlds had collided.

'It's so beautiful,' Aunty Jane murmured.

'What is?' I asked, although I was nodding my head at the street in front of us.

'Life,' Aunty Jane said. 'I know it's easy to get down, but remember, at the end of the day, there is still a lot of good, a lot to look forward to.'

I shrugged. I knew she was right, but trying to think positively some days was a lot harder than others.

Tommy and Jack also had their hearings in the Children's Court. Tommy faced several more counts than Jack, not only with regard to what he did to Annie, but also the stuff the cops accessed on his computer — charges relating to child pornography. He got twelve months' detention, but with allowances and concessions — I'm not sure exactly. The most time he would serve would be six months.

It doesn't seem like a lot in retrospect, but at the time no one could believe that we would face prison. Least of all Jack — that's what he told me when I visited him in detention. But he got a month for his part in it.

'My lawyer was so surprised,' Jack said across the metal tabletop. He looked so bad, so small and grey. 'She didn't think I'd get any time at all. Community service, that kind of stuff. But the judge was furious, said this behaviour was a scourge on society. That we were out of control. That this kind of behaviour had to be stopped. An example.' He shrugged defeatedly. And that was it, he looked defeated.

'What's it like?' I asked. When he looked at me I knew then that something had been broken inside him. Irretrievably broken. He looked me squarely in the eye, yet it was like he was seeing straight through me. Seeing something, or many things, that he wished he had never seen.

'I can't lie to you, Jazz,' he reached across and held my hand so tightly I swear I thought he was going to pulverise my bones. 'It's a living nightmare.' He pushed a lock of hair out of his eyes and grimaced. 'I know I've got what I deserve, probably less than what I deserve. When I think about what we did. And I think about her, alone in a hospital room, not being able to breathe for herself. I guess that's the real nightmare. But fuck, Jazz, if I could turn back time I would in a heartbeat, just to never see what I've had to see or do here.'

Things ran through my mind. Hollywood TV shows about male prison — knifings, fights, drugs, and the other ... the one that made me cringe (don't worry, the irony is apparent) — rape. Had Jack been raped in there? 'Like what?'

He shook his head. 'I can't tell you. It's best you don't know. But whatever you're imagining, knowing you as well as I do, you're probably right.'

I listened to his words and realised he was wrong. We didn't know each other well at all. That too had been destroyed. He was still Jack, but he'd never be *my* Jack ever again. When I used to think about the future, Jack was always in it, always my go-to guy. I'd imagined we'd go to uni, we'd always socialise together, one day he'd get a girl and I'd be best man at his wedding. But now, looking at the hollowed-out shell of who he was — the flimsy photocopy where the ink had faded in lines, blurring edges and details — I realised that was never going to happen. That we had killed that too.

'Where's Tommy?' I asked after we had sat for a while in that awkward silence where no one can think of a thing to say.

'In a different section,' Jack said, 'under protection, really.'

'Why?' I asked surprised.

'Because he's a fucking dog,' Jack spat, and in those words the enormity of the change was apparent. The tone, the jargon, words my Jack would never have used before in his life — *a dog*. He sounded so, so, criminal. 'Others in here know about him. He came in the big man, boasting about his achievements, what he'd done, why he'd done it.'

'Why?' I asked, genuinely interested in the answer. 'Why *did* he do it?' It was something that had plagued me from the beginning of the whole Greenheadgate saga. What had compelled Tommy to post those photos and upload that video? He'd never been the smartest kid in the class, but that was so dumb. Even a ten-year-old would know they were incriminating themselves with such hardcore evidence. Why did he do it?

'Attention,' Jack said staring over my shoulder. 'Kudos. Feeling important. He told me after we were arrested that's why he did it — because he could. He didn't care about the consequences. He said his mum was such a bitch, he could see why his dad had pretty much permanently fucked off — so why not? Who would care what he did, he was leaving Greenhead anyway. He said chicks deserved it. If only I'd listened to you, Jazz.'

'Me?' I said, 'what do you mean?'

'Ages ago you said there was something wrong about him. You were right.'

'It doesn't matter now,' I said.

'No, it doesn't. I'm in here for a month. Tommy is being protected because he's been beaten pretty badly and some of the guys in here would be happy to see him dead.'

'Dead,' I said. 'Seriously?'

'This isn't holiday camp, Jazz. Some of the kids in here have committed serious crimes — like one guy killed both his mother and father over a fight about some biscuits, or some shit. Tommy thought he was the big man but he had no idea how fucking puny he is.'

'They've turned Annie off.' There, I'd finally said the words I'd come to tell him. I watched him go that sickly shade of green-grey again, like he did that time the video came through .

'Fuck,' he put his head into his shaking hands.

'She's alive,' I said softly. His head snapped up and he glared at me. Really hatefully — a look I'd never seen before. A look that belonged to this new Jack.

'You waited all this time to tell me?'

'I *came* here to tell you,' I said angrily.

'You let me talk about the shit in here when you could have told me straight away. The one thing I've waited for all this time. The one thing I needed to know. I needed to hear. To know that it'd all be alright.'

And like you, dear reader, that was all I heard as well. I, I, I, me, me, me. How this would impact upon Jack. Jack's ability to leave this place and live his life without the knowledge that he'd contributed to the death of someone. It made all his remorse and tears look like bullshit. This new version of Jack was someone I didn't care to know at all.

I stood up.

'Wait, Jazz,' he put out his hand again. I noticed the bitten fingernails where the skin was broken and bleeding, a habit Jack had overcome at the start of Year 8, when he used to bite and pluck at the skin on his thumbs until they were red and swollen and bleeding. 'Is she okay?'

I shrugged. 'I don't know. They switched her off knowing she would breathe. I don't know if she's brain-damaged or not. No one does.'

'Fuck,' he sighed.

'I'm going.' I wanted to get out. I hadn't expected it to be like this. I'd gone in to speak to Jack, not this shady replica of him. He gave me the creeps. I didn't trust him.

'Jazz, will you come back?' Jack asked. 'I know it's not long, but I need all the support I can get.'

'Sure,' I said, knowing full well I'd never go back there again.

Post 31: The women's refuge

It was a house not unlike Aunty Jane's and it was only two blocks away. That first morning I told Aunty Jane I'd walk there, but she didn't seem convinced.

'Do you want me to walk with you?' she asked as we finished our coffees. I shook my head. It was another beautiful day. I watched the light flit through the leaves of the huge gum tree in the backyard as they wavered lightly in the breeze.

'No,' I said, 'thanks, but I think I need to do this part on my own.' I'd lain awake most of the night, unable to turn my racing brain off. This was the punishment I'd been given for my part in the whole affair. Everyone else was facing (or had faced) their punishments alone, and I knew I had to as well. I couldn't rely on my aunt for everything. At some point I had to grow up and accept responsibility. A part of me also thought that maybe this would be it, that facing my punishment alone would be a way of signing off on the night of Greenheadgate.

Despite my convictions, I've got to admit I was terribly nervous as I walked down the street. I wasn't sure what I would find. During the night I'd googled the organisation that runs the refuge and read up on its services and objectives. It provided crisis relief to women trying to escape violent and abusive relationships. The address of my specific refuge had been given to me over the phone by their Volunteer Coordinator but was nowhere online, to protect the women's safety, and I had signed a confidentiality agreement that really emphasised the need to protect people's information. It never properly occurred to me before that information had such power.

I walked in the front door. It was the entrance hall of the original house and a young woman emerged from a back room. She was wiping her hands with a tea towel, and gave me a somewhat reserved smile. 'Can I help you?' she asked.

'Hi,' I said, my mouth dry, 'I'm Jasmine and I'm here to do some volunteer work.'

'Right,' she said, neither friendly nor hostile. It made me even more nervous. 'Come through here.' She led the way into the kitchen, where the sink was full of hot suds. 'You wash and I'll dry.'

I nodded and started washing up the cups, placing them on the drainer for her to dry. 'My name's Carol,' she said, 'and I'm full-time here.' I nodded silently. I didn't know what to say, what to ask, or even what to volunteer. 'I saw that this is court-ordered,' Carol said.

I glanced at her. Again, I couldn't read her face and wasn't sure whether she was being disapproving or not. 'Yes,' I said, 'I got into a bit of trouble and this was what the judge ordered me to do.'

'Well, I'm glad you're here,' Carol said and I glanced her way again. This time she smiled at me. 'A lot of people never fulfil their orders.'

'Really?' I was amazed. 'Even if a court demands it?' Who on earth would disobey a judge?

'Yes, I hear about it all the time. In fact, in this place you hear about a lot of things that are unbelievable. To me, the fact you came indicates you really are remorseful for what you've done.' It had never occurred to me that I might not fulfil my punishment. As far as I was concerned, not going would have led to more trouble, and the last thing I wanted was any more of that.

'It's a difficult system, see,' Carol continued to talk as she put the cups away. 'There's not enough money or help. We rely on volunteers and donations to keep the place going. Government funding is constantly cut, yet the incidence of domestic abuse is on the rise. Come through here.' She led the way to a laundry out the back of the property. Two large washers were at work. 'We'll fold these,' she pointed to a mountain of bed linen. 'The situation is that one woman dies every week in Australia at the hands of her partner or ex-partner.' Her words chilled me.

'Really?' I said. 'That's so many.'

'It is,' Carol agreed, 'but the problem is they have nowhere to go, so they stay as the violence escalates. Or they have a VRO in place, but the partner just ignores it and returns to the home. It's difficult to follow up on and often, when the partner doesn't show in court but hasn't reoffended, the system lets it slide.'

'What's a VRO?' I asked.

'Violence Restraining Order — it's court-issued and prevents a person being within a certain distance of another,' Carol said.

'And these men just ignore it?' It seemed outrageous. Where was the protection?

'Yes,' she nodded, 'often there's drugs and alcohol involved, and sometimes when that's the case all reason and logic is gone.' Her words resonated with me. I'd experienced that exact thing. 'We've got ten beds here, and they're always full, but this accommodation is crisis — which means only temporary — so we try to get counselling and help while they're here and then find them somewhere safe to go.'

'So, what's a day like here?' I asked. I was starting to warm to Carol, who, despite her aloofness, seemed to genuinely care.

'They vary. It's pretty much all centred on making the women feel safe. At some point there'll be a form of counselling, whether formal, group or informal. But the women are not pushed to share their stories — it's very much about offering a refuge, a haven, while other plans can be made.'

I folded the linen silently. 'Can I ask you something?'

Carol nodded, 'Sure.'

'Why do you do it?' I asked. While I could see the importance of such a place, it'd have to be depressing. All these battered women, emotionally or physically, rocking up and seeking help.

'Like most people involved in a place like this, I have my own story,' Carol led me to an outdoor table and chairs and indicated for me to sit down. 'I escaped an abusive relationship about ten years ago. My ex-husband wasn't physical, he was emotionally abusive. Living with him was like walking on eggshells — I know it's such a cliché, but it describes exactly that feeling. Creeping around, hoping not to do anything to get noticed, making yourself smaller and less visible, because you know that if you cause displeasure, the consequences aren't worth it. Sometimes it's raised voices, sometimes it's stony silence. And it's so insidious, you don't know it's even happening. It starts small — terse comments about something inadequate, maybe once I asked him to stop on his way home for milk and then when he walked in the door he was sullen, ignoring me. When I asked if everything was alright he just turned around and pretended I wasn't there, as if I wasn't actually talking to him. Nothing to really complain about, but the first level in creating anxiety about asking him to do things. And then the boundaries get shifted further out. He once offered to mind the children for an hour so I could pick something up. When I was delayed — it wasn't ready — I could feel my anxiety increasing. Two hours later when I returned home he was furious. He looked at me full of contempt, narrowed his eyes and said he couldn't believe how useless I was.'

'But he'd offered to help you.' This was starting to feel familiar to me.

'Oh yeah,' Carol shrugged, 'but within his terms. His control. One hour blew out into two and he wasn't happy — so he made sure I wasn't happy too. And because the details for each incident seem so trivial, you don't talk about it. He didn't act like that in front of others. In fact he was always the opposite. Mr Generosity — until it didn't go his way, and then I would hear about it. I would suffer for what someone else had done, suddenly every single thing he was unhappy about was my fault. By the end he didn't really care about hiding that dark side from our friends. We'd be out at dinner with people and he'd make snide comments and put me down in front of everyone. It made me feel so small, so humiliated, that I stopped accepting invitations. I decided it was easier not to socialise than face the embarrassment of it all. I became totally isolated. It got to the point where I realised the situation had stripped me of my identity. I felt totally worthless. Powerless. I had nowhere to go. No family here. I had no money of my own — he controlled that — no job prospects. I felt trapped, and the more insignificant I grew the more powerful he became. It felt like only a matter of time before something would break. I just lived in fear.'

As Carol was speaking I suddenly realised why it felt so familiar. I saw a lot of my own father in the ex-husband she described. A powerful and controlling force. The way my mother crept around him, placating him, ensuring that nothing displeased him. Including me. I had to wonder whether my father was also guilty of domestic abuse.

I stayed at the shelter for two hours and helped

prepare the morning tea. I watched the women rise and come into the living areas. I listened to their chatter. Some of them smiled at me as they passed by. None of them sported any bruises or physical damage to their faces, none of them looked haggard or distressed. They carried their injuries on the inside. They looked like regular, normal, everyday women who you see on the bus, at the shops, down the beach. And that's when I realised the insidious nature of it all: they *were* the women I saw every day.

'It's scary,' I told Aunty Jane later that day. 'When I realise the extent of it. It's not that battered woman on the front of an awareness brochure, it's anyone.'

'Yes,' Aunty Jane agreed. 'I guess all relationships are about power. And it's a matter of getting the balance right because when there is a huge discrepancy the one with the power has all the control. When do you go back?'

'Next Saturday,' I said. 'I'm just doing dishes and folding stuff, helping make food, that kind of thing. It's not as bad as I thought.'

I did my time there, and by the end of it I was kind of sad to go. Carol had turned out to be a good support — she had a huge heart and it was clear, through everything she did, that her only goal was to make the women feel safe. I got to know a few of them, but their stories aren't mine to share. What I learnt from them was the importance of being an individual, of not tying yourself so completely to another person that you couldn't extract yourself. Always having options. Some of them regretted their lack of education, others — highly qualified women — had been tied by religious or cultural beliefs, some by finances, others by children and the fear of splitting up the family. But by the end of my ten hours there they had all said the same thing: that no one should live in fear, that no one should feel at the mercy of another, that everyone has the right to freedom and happiness.

Post 32: *Let me be frank*

Dear reader, I'm sorry that it's been a while since we last met. Something got in the way of my blogging and it's called life. Yes, I hope you will be happy to hear (depending on your overall opinion of me) that my life has moved on and, as usual, my Aunty Jane was right — there is a lot to look forward to. But today an event occurred that took me back to Greenhead (mentally, not physically — I hope to never, ever set foot in that miserable town again), which reminded me of the whole sordid affair, but also put into perspective my life over the last two years.

   The telling of that chance encounter will have to wait a few posts longer though, while I bring you up to date.

Let me start with Frank. I have to be the luckiest girl on the planet to have hooked myself such a hottie. So what did you know about him? Not much, I guess. When I met Frank — remember *that* incident? — I thought he was just a crazy barista. In a way he really is crazy — he loves me! I know, I'm sounding all girlish and silly, but Frank has done so much for my self-esteem. I've been so lucky to have his love and support. After my first shift with him, I started working Saturdays and Sundays. Chicco was always busy, filled with an alternative crowd who'd sit around debating world issues, vehemently arguing their case while small maltese terriers, beagles and sausage dogs curled at their feet sleeping. Frank ran the show. Not only was he a top-rate barista (and I'm pleased to say it's something I've added to my own skills list), he knew how to charm the ladies and chat sports, politics and religion with the gents. Chicco was known for having the best coffee on the strip (it's true — it was formally awarded by the City of Vincent). But more so, it was known for great service, relaxed ambiance and the hospitality of Frank.

As well as being a barista, Frank is also a

musician. And not just any musician — Frank is actually Nials Wisher. Some of you will be gasping for air right now — well, those of you who are under thirty and listen to Triple J. Yes, Nials Wisher is my Frank Adamo, who is also number twenty-seven on iTunes at the moment.

So now, dear reader, if you'll indulge me, I'd like to take you back in time.

We were at Chicco and it was late. We'd closed and I was pretty sure I had BO. It had been a mad day — North Perth had a food festival on and we were inundated with tourists (by tourists I mean people from outside the suburb). I was sitting at a table, surreptitiously sniffing the shirt under my armpit, when Frank plonked two coffees and a piece of cheesecake in front of me.

'Cheesecake, my favourite,' I said.

'Mine too,' Frank picked up a spoon, 'but only the traditional type.'

'Agreed,' I dug into the side of it, 'not those horrible baked ones.'

'Ugh,' Frank said, 'they're not cheesecakes.'

'Agreed,' I agreed again, marvelling at our

similarities (but at that point I had no idea how deep they ran). 'So how come you work here?'

'Well,' Frank dragged the cheesecake off his fork with his wonderfully white teeth, 'money, mostly. But also, it's the family business, and you do what you do for family.' I nearly choked. Frank was an Adamo? Of the Adamo fortune? The Adamos, an Italian family who migrated to Australia after World War II, had created a coffee empire in North Perth. Their coffee shops — Chicco being the flagship — numbered over forty across the country. But they weren't a franchise. They were a family-run business, and believe me, the Adamos were an extensive, extended family.

I spluttered cheesecake. 'You're an Adamo?' I squeaked.

'Guilty,' Frank said, 'but while coffee is the family business, my passion lies in music.'

'A musician too?' I remember not believing that this guy was real. Who could be that hot, rich and level? Not even in a Disney film.

'I play,' Frank said, 'and I'm working on a new way to fuse jazz and rock. I don't know what to call it though.'

'You should call it jock,' I said. He laughed loudly.

'Perfect, but for the fact that no jock will listen to it. It's really more for the ladies.'

'Razz?' I ventured.

'Even better.' Frank stood. 'Can I play you something?'

I nodded. I've always been supremely impressed by people who can play music. Frank emerged from the kitchen with an acoustic guitar. 'Normally I plug into a machine, which records me, then I loop it back and use it as my backing, or my band, if you like. It's kind of experimental. But jazz requires certain instruments — like a sax, which I don't play. So this way I can synthesise my sounds and have a range of different-sounding instruments behind me.'

I won't go into detail about what he played that night, but those of you who know Nials Wisher will know exactly what I heard. It was mesmerising, and (like his eyes, I've got to admit) a bit enchanting.

'It's beautiful,' I said, his melody lodged in my head. But more than that were his words, his lyrics. The man was a modern-day poet. 'I love it.'

'Thank you,' Frank smiled and looked up at me

from his guitar. 'I've got a gig next weekend, and a couple of people from here are going. Would you like to come?'

'Is it at a pub? I'm not eighteen,' I said.

'Oh, I'm sure that won't be a problem, I know the owner. But you won't be able to drink.'

I shook my head, 'Fine with me.' And it was. Following Greenheadgate I'd vowed I'd never drink again.

The gig was at a small bar called The Stoned Crow tucked down an alleyway in the heart of Northbridge. Frank picked me up from Aunty Jane's with Tony from Chicco and Lisa, Tony's girlfriend. They were all eighteen, so I was feeling a bit out of my depth and wondering why I had agreed to go to this gig. It was midweek so I didn't expect there to be many people, but the place was buzzing. Frank found us a table near the stage.

'Back in a sec,' he said, dumping his gear on the floor. I sat at the table feeling a bit awkward, until Tony started talking about the crazy cat lady who came into Chicco at least twice a day.

'So, she's convinced that we have no right

running a coffee shop in the middle of a residential area,' Tony said.

'But Chicco has been there for fifty years,' I said.

'Right — she's had this belief for that long — it's just as time has gone by, and all the other coffee shops have sprung up, she thinks it's all Joe's fault,' Tony said. 'So today she comes in to warn us that she's put a hex on the coffee shop and all its employees.'

'Great,' I said, 'what's going to happen to us?'

'She wouldn't say,' Tony said, 'but Frank came out, tried to calm her down and get her out.'

'Did she go?' I asked.

'Yeah,' Tony said, 'you know what Frank is like. A real charmer. Gave her a kilo of coffee beans and a pie, told her how lovely she was looking and managed to get her to lift the hex.'

'Seriously?' I said.

'Yep,' Tony said. 'Speak of the devil.' I watched Frank make his way through the crowd to us.

'All good?' Frank looked at me. I nodded. 'I'm up next,' he said and pointed to the stage where a long-haired girl was sitting on a stool with an acoustic guitar. She reminded me of Jenny from *Forrest Gump*.

'She's so pretty,' I said to no one in particular.

'She's got an awesome voice. Her name is Tahlia Newton — and I'm pretty sure she's about to be discovered,' Frank said. 'Wait til she starts, you've never heard anything like it.'

He was right, she had that ethereal, warbling sound that made English sound like a slightly different language.

'She's so good,' I said, clapping loudly as she finished her set. Frank looked pleased.

'Well, if you like her, you might like me then. There's hope for me yet,' he stood up and picked up his guitar. 'Give us a hand, Tony?'

'No worries, bro,' Tony said, picking up Frank's amp. They moved to the stage where Tahlia was standing to receive the applause and whistles of the crowd. Lisa leaned towards me.

'It's so nice to finally meet you,' she said. 'Frank has told me so much about you.'

'You mean Tony,' I corrected her. Why would Frank talk about me? 'I mostly work with Tony.'

'Yes,' Lisa nodded, 'Tony has mentioned you, but not as much as Frank.' She smiled, 'I'm so glad you came on a date with him.'

'Date?' I laughed loudly. 'This isn't a date. Frank just invited me to come to listen to him play. It's just a thing.'

Lisa frowned, 'Oh, I thought ...' and then she was muffled by the applause of the crowd as Frank took the stage. He had taken his leather jacket off and stood with his shirt rolled up above his elbows, tight black jeans and narrow leather shoes. I couldn't help but think how hot he was.

'Thanks for coming,' he said. 'My name is Nials Wisher and I'm going to play a couple of tunes for you.' He started strumming his guitar and clicking a few pedals on the floor, and then the music he'd played for me at the coffee shop suddenly took on magnificent proportions. He had the full backing of other instruments and his own voice was harmonising with his pre-recording. There was one man on stage, with a guitar, but the effect was that of an entire jazz band. It was awesome.

'He's amazing,' Lisa said. I nodded. I'd never heard anything like him. His voice, his lyrics. Sitting there I realised that my crush had suddenly gone epic. I was totally fangirling him.

'Nials Wisher?' I asked as he approached the table.

He laughed. 'Yeah, it was something that started a while ago. I didn't want to perform as an Adamo — in case I wasn't good enough and spoilt the family rep, or if I succeeded people would think it was only because I was an Adamo. Neither has happened, but the name has stuck,' he shrugged. 'It's kind of cool in a way — when I get up there I truly become a different person. It makes it easy to handle the criticism.'

'What criticism?' I asked. 'The crowd love you.'

'This crowd does,' Frank said, 'but I've played in places where they've hated me.' He lifted his fringe up and there was a long scar. 'Some guy hated me so much he threw a bottle at my head. Thirteen stitches.'

'Oh my god,' I shook my head. 'Yet you came back for more?'

'Yep,' Frank said. 'I'll never perform there again, of course. But when you love something enough, you always pursue it.'

I nodded. Frank was so inspiring. When he dropped me home I realised that things had started to improve. I had been out — not on a date, as Lisa had thought, but out with a group. My days of isolation might be ending, I thought. There was a chance that I might have friends again.

Post 33: Learning trust

And so the days passed, a mix of study and work. I feel like work is the wrong word for my time at Chicco, I loved it so much. I loved the regulars, who would drop in for a chat and whose orders I always knew in advance. I loved the staff. And I loved Joe, Frank's dad, who was always making me take home pastry and cake for my family.

'You take this to your aunty,' Joe would say, wrapping up a homemade beef pie and an apple strudel. 'She feeds the many.'

I'd given up refusing. 'Let me pay,' I pleaded with him, 'you can't pay me *and* give me stuff.'

Joe looked at me with those same dark eyes Frank had. 'It's to show my gratitude,' Joe said. 'If it wasn't for the loyalty of your aunty I wouldn't have my finest employee. I never forget a good turn.' It was easy to see where Frank got his charm from.

And of course working at Chicco meant spending time with Frank. Our coffee and cake had become a weekly occurrence, and most shifts we were on together. The rare times I turned up and Frank wasn't there were the only times it ever felt remotely like work. But the next time Frank would be there, leaning against the counter and smiling at me when I walked in the door.

'Morning, Shiraz. Miss me yesterday?' he'd ask, and I'd shake my head at him.

'Not really, didn't even realise you weren't here,' I'd say, tying my apron on.

One day I was filling the pastry cabinet and Frank was chatting to a tall raven-haired girl with deep chocolate-coloured eyes. Even I thought she was beautiful, so I wasn't surprised to see Frank's charm offensive was switched to high. And because I had such a huge crush on him by then, I have to admit I was feeling somewhat jealous. She was flirting back with him.

'So,' she drawled with obvious confidence, 'how

much longer do I have to wait, Frank?'

'I'm pretty sure you don't ever have to wait for anything, Layla,' Frank said, fashioning a love heart onto her coffee.

'Well, you've been keeping me waiting for a year,' she pouted.

'Have I?' Frank pushed the coffee across, his hand brushing hers. I was mesmerised by this ritual. Peering at them through the glass cabinet, I wished I were Layla. 'What am I withholding from you?' he said.

'You,' she pouted. 'I decided that if you didn't finally ask me on a date today then I would ask you.'

'Oh,' Frank rushed around the counter and grabbed Layla's hands. She giggled prettily. 'Layla, I will fall on my sword if I've misled you into thinking that I was going to ask you on a date. In fact, this is a good opportunity for me to reassess my behaviour, because I am madly in love with someone and I would die if she perceived me as a womaniser or outrageous flirt still.'

Layla looked shocked. As Frank had suggested, I'm sure Layla had never had to wait for anything, or not get what she wanted. 'Hmmm,' Layla said, 'so the word *still* indicates that there were signs there? That I've not made this all up?'

'Ah Layla,' Frank murmured, 'it's true. I think up until recently I may have sent you the wrong signals — I was so in awe of your beauty. But one doesn't choose for the heart. The heart chooses. And mine has.'

I waited for Layla's reaction. Frank had the type of sincerity and humour that somehow made these crazy expressions sound thoughtful and kind.

'Who is she?' Layla asked. I thought she was handling the rejection gracefully — but then again, she was graceful in all ways.

'My Shiraz,' Frank said, looking at me.

I was so surprised I banged my head into the shelf and a strawberry cheesecake fell onto the floor, splatting over my boots and up my trouser legs.

'Shit,' I muttered reaching down to pick it up.

'Look at her, Layla, don't you agree she's beautiful, graceful and elegant?' Frank quipped, and I couldn't tell if he was serious or just having a laugh. I straightened, my cheeks burning red, crumbs in my plait and my hands full of berries and cream cheese.

'Hi,' I said and stared at Frank. And then I saw

it. He was looking at me in a way I'd only ever seen once before. And that was the way Uncle Rob looked at Aunty Jane. 'Frank?'

'Tell me you feel the same?' Frank came back behind the counter and grabbed my mucky hands, 'because I have to confess I used every weapon I had to get you here. The day of the coffee scam, I used a secret family recipe that we don't even sell here, in order to win that debate, and win you.'

'Vanilla?' I asked, laughing. 'I've never tasted it since.'

'Correct,' Frank was also laughing. 'Agree to go out with me, on a real date, and I'll even share that secret with you.'

'Who could resist that?' I said, shaking my head.

'Not me,' said Layla. 'You're a lucky girl. What did you do to deserve him?'

And then those words sent me into a panic. What *had* I done to deserve him? Nothing. I'd ruined another girl's life. How could I admit that to this beautiful man? My secret past would be revealed if I went on a date with him. So far I'd evaded personal talk at work, redirecting our conversations to the world we lived in, not the sordid past I'd escaped. I wouldn't be able to hide it any longer and then this new Jazz, Frank's own Shiraz, would be exposed. The façade would crumble and he'd never see me the same way again. I felt like I was suffocating. 'Oh hang on,' I said untying my apron, 'I've just remembered I've got to go.' Both Frank and Layla looked at me bewildered.

'Jazz?' Frank said, putting out a hand as if to stop me. 'Are you okay?'

'Sorry,' I was trying not to flip out, but I could barely contain my panic. 'I know my shift isn't over but I've got to go.'

I ran.

I sat in my room shaking. How would it ever be possible to move on from the wreckage I'd created? The policewoman's words still haunted me: 'They will never leave you alone. When you don't suspect it, they will reappear and you'll be facing this judgement again.' How would I ever be accepted again by normal people once they knew the truth about me?

Aunty Jane tapped on my door. 'You're home early,' she said, 'is everything okay?'

'Everything is terrible,' I confessed. 'I ran out on Frank. I can't ever go back there. I can't face him and tell him the truth about me. I feel like a liar and a phony. I can't escape what I've done. Ever.'

'He's here,' Aunty Jane said, nodding towards the house.

'Here? Who is? Frank?' I was in a terrible panic.

'He's worried he's offended you. Overstepped the boundaries. He thinks he's scared you. He doesn't look happy,' she admitted.

'Oh shit,' I ran my hands through my hair and crumbs fell out. 'What am I going to do?'

'Talk to him,' Aunty Jane said.

'And tell him what?' I wanted to cry. I wanted to scream. 'Tell him I raped my best friend, and then abandoned her? That I've been disowned by my parents? That I have a criminal conviction? I can't. I can't do it,' I was rambling and panicking and rambling.

'Just tell him the truth, honey,' Aunty Jane said. 'If he doesn't like it he can leave. You can quit your job. Or, he might just surprise you.'

I followed Aunty Jane into the house. I still had my work uniform on. My hair was out and it was a mess. I felt feral. Frank leapt to his feet when he saw me.

'Jazz, I'm so sorry,' he said, looking forlorn. 'I've made a massive dick of myself. I've embarrassed you publicly. I know how shy and reserved you are.'

Shy and reserved? That surprised me — was that what he saw?

He continued. 'I wasn't planning on doing that. I wanted to wait until we'd shut shop and sat down for a coffee and cheesecake.' He looked at my splattered pants. 'Although maybe not the strawberry one. But I was going to tell you how much I loved your company and our chats, how funny and clever you are. How beautiful I think you are. And I didn't want you to think that I was the old flirt still. I still love the ladies, but I wanted to tell you that there is only one for me and I wanted to ask you out. On a real date, so that this time you'd know it was one — not like last time.' He finally paused for breath and looked at me expectantly.

'I would go out with you in a heartbeat,' I said, and the truth actually felt good. 'It's just that there is so much you don't know about me. I wasn't always shy and reserved. It's just been since I got here, from the country. I had to leave some really bad stuff behind, stuff that I didn't want to tell anyone. Because of what a terrible person I've been.'

'Maybe,' Frank moved closer, 'you could give me a chance? You could try and tell me what happened — whatever you're comfortable telling me. And see what happens?'

'I think you'll hate me,' I said.

He was shaking his head. 'I'm pretty sure I won't,' Frank said. 'Will you trust me?'

I nodded. I had to start somewhere.

Frank drove us to the beach. It was a warm evening and we sat on the sand, our feet bare, and I told him about the party, the abuse and then everything that followed, including Annie's suicide attempt and the court case. I couldn't look at him. I stared at the sun settling down on the horizon. 'So that's it. The truth about what a terrible person I am.'

'This is the bit you miss,' Frank said. He picked up my hand and I felt electricity run up my arm. 'A truly terrible person wouldn't think they were terrible. They would justify their actions, place all the blame on others. But you don't, Jazz, you remind yourself all the time that you did this awful thing. I think you need to realise you made a drunken mistake, one that had massive consequences. You know, as you were talking I was thinking of all the stupid things I've ever done, drunk and sober, and what the effects could have been. But I was lucky. You were caught up in a whole string of effects.'

I sighed heavily. 'Really? Do you really believe that?'

'Yes,' he threaded his fingers through mine. 'I know the real Jazz. I know that inside is a beautiful girl who matches her beautiful exterior. You are lovely, you know.'

'Well, that's what my birth certificate says,' I said.

Frank laughed. 'And funny, too. Can we go on a real date?' He turned his brown eyes on me and I think they were hypnotic or magical because I nodded my head.

'Yes.'

Post 34: Lattes are for skinny cows

A couple of months ago, I had my final high school exams.

I sat them at the Central TAFE with other external students. My studies had been hard over the years following Greenheadgate, but I was a motivated student. No matter what had happened, I couldn't allow this to be a fuck-up too. So I'd studied late into each evening when Aunty Jane and the kids were asleep. I'd pored over my textbooks, memorising dates and formulas, theories and concepts. I'd kept meticulous files with highlighted notes, colour-coded in terms of importance, or relevance. I'd reread the English texts more than fifteen times — to this day I can still quote verbatim F. Scott Fitzgerald or Virginia Woolf. I was so prepared. By studying I'd allowed myself to retreat from the horrors of that night and replace them with a hope that somehow, someday, I might be able to move on past that dirty and sordid pivotal moment in my life. And of course I also had work and Frank.

But, as I am wont to do, I digress. I was at the exam room waiting for the examiner to open the doors when I saw Casey. She was sitting with a group of girls, also waiting to go in. Her long blonde hair, pulled back into a high ponytail, glinted in the sun as she was regaling them with some story. It was when she stopped laughing that her eyes darted across the courtyard and she saw me. I think the look was shock, then surprise, and I realised I was holding my breath until she smiled at me. It was a genuine and warm welcoming smile that showed me without doubt she didn't have the same scorn and derision I imagined those back at Namba High had for me. I watched her excuse herself and come over to me, a slight skip in her step.

'Is that a lovely Jasmine Lovely I see before me?' she said, opening her arms. We embraced and I pulled back to look at her. Since my self-imposed exile I had not run into one person from that world.

I had removed Facebook and Snapchat from my life when I'd removed Jack from it. There was nothing good to be had from sitting hundreds of kilometres away and watching the actions of people you formerly knew. I'd made my exile complete once I'd found out that Annie had survived. The need to know, which had once driven me, I'd driven from me. And though I created this blog after I left Greenhead, I've never tagged any real names, and no one from Namba has ever commented nor tried to get in touch with me via it. I had no idea what anyone there was up to.

'How are you?' Casey asked.

'Good. Nervous,' I said, and then I was automatically embarrassed — she might think I meant nervous about seeing her. I waved a hand to the exam room. 'Exams.'

'I know,' she nodded. 'Lit.'

'Why are you here?' I asked.

'I left Namba, after you did,' she said as the examiner opened the doors. 'I couldn't stand that small town — full of small-minded people. I've been studying Distance Ed — travelling with my father.' She nodded to remind me. 'He's in the Army.'

I too nodded, as though I remembered, but truthfully I had fairly erased that type of information from my memory. 'So we're in town for the exams, then off to Dubai for a few months. And you?'

I shook my head. I didn't want to sit down and recount all my post-Greenhead life. 'Distance Ed too.' I pointed to the door. 'We've got to go in.'

'Sure,' she said and linked her arm through mine. 'How about we catch up after — in three hours we'll probably want a latte, we can go to Skinny Cow.'

I nodded, despite the overwhelming urge to flee. 'Sure,' I agreed. I was a staunch Chicco supporter — but I wasn't taking Casey there.

We sat across from each other in the coffee shop. I had a skinny latte and Casey a long black. She seemed so mature, sophisticated, older. But when I reflect on it, that was always her distinguishing feature — her ability to rise above everyone else, not get caught up in other people's dramas.

'What do you want to know?' she asked me after we had exchanged pleasantries and the unavoidable finally came up. It had to. My whole life since Greenheadgate had been shaped by that one event.

Where I was now and what I was doing was a direct consequence of that night — so it was inevitable that we would go over everything.

'How is Annie?' I squeezed my eyes shut for a moment. Saying her name had made me feel light-headed and slightly queasy. I looked suspiciously at my coffee.

'They made the decision to turn off life support because she was recovering,' Casey said, filling in all the blanks no one else could. 'The doctors told her parents that Annie could sustain her own life, without assistance. But when her cousins were posting it on Facebook they wanted people to think she was going to die. They wanted to punish you.'

'Me?' I asked.

'And Tommy and Jack. They were furious with the sentences. There was a lot of turmoil in town over the fairness, or lack thereof, depending on which side you were on. They knew she would survive, but what they didn't know was at what cost.'

'And?' The dread overwhelmed me. I wanted the outcome to be good, of course I did. My culpability was enormous.

'She's changed,' Casey said gently. She hesitated

when she saw the tears in my eyes, but I waved her on. I couldn't protect myself from the truth, and I didn't want to. I guess I needed the punishment too. 'At first it looked like she would never speak again, but slowly she has learnt to read and write.'

'Oh God,' I said.

'They say she has the intellect of about a nine-year-old. But she is happy and learning every day. Who knows?' Casey said optimistically.

I thought of my friend Annie, the girl with the wicked sense of humour and a talent for acting. I thought of the laughs we used to share, the secrets we told each other, the experiences we'd had. That girl was gone. And now she was someone else. And this was what we had done.

'I feel sick,' I looked at my coffee and willed what I'd sipped not to come up. 'This is my fault.'

Casey nodded. 'Jazz, I'm not going to blow smoke up your arse. You're too smart for that. You were a part of it. But we all were.'

'I was a major part,' I said angrily, but not at Casey — at myself. Of all the times I'd wished I could change things, at that point I'd never wished it harder.

'We all were,' Casey said again. 'The way we all

behaved. The things we did and said. The times we were so drunk and acting stupidly. I, more than others, get that. Most of us were luckier than you and Jack — even Tommy. We all did things like what you did that night but we got away with it.' I nodded. This was exactly what Frank had spent the last two years convincing me of. But it was still hard to accept — even now. Especially now.

'And now I'm sitting my exams. I'm getting on with my life, I've got an awesome boyfriend, I'm planning on studying and travelling, and what has she got?' I could hear my anger with myself rising again. 'Fucking Crayolas and My Little Pony.'

'Yes,' Casey nodded, 'but she also has a family who loves and supports her. Who are there for her.' Casey held my eyes for the longest time. 'Sometimes other people have things we don't.'

'It makes me so mad,' I said tiredly. 'How can I go into the next exam and try my hardest when Annie doesn't even get that opportunity?'

'How can you not?' Casey said. 'How can you not try your hardest? Seriously, Jazz, how many casualties do there have to be? At some point you have to move on and let go — I know, I feel like I'm singing the Disney song from *Frozen*, but it's true.'

I nodded. I agreed with her, but the idea of making my life better when I had all but totally destroyed Annie's made me sick to my very core — and sure that I would never, ever totally recover from what I'd done that night.

I made it through the rest of the exams fairly easily. Like I said, I was well prepared. What I wasn't prepared for were the waves of nausea that continued to wash over me when I was least expecting it, especially in the middle of the Calculus exam. It was fear, dread and self-loathing bundled with an indescribable sadness. I had never felt so dreadfully sad in my life before. I guess it was the reality, the final outcome, the last consequence. No one had gotten off freely. Jack had finished his month in detention and returned home to Greenhead, a totally different boy to the one who entered its doors before. I heard from Aunty Jane, who kept in contact with my mother (more on that later), that Maria said he was now harder and more introverted. The prankster had gone, replaced with a steely coldness. There were no more jokes from

Jack, he had finished with his loose approach to life. He didn't stay in Greenhead long, couldn't settle, and even though his parents remained there he was now living with his grandmother. I didn't wish anything but happiness for Jack — I couldn't change the fundamental affection I'd always had for him — but I knew there was no place in my life for him. It would always be a constant reminder of our stupidity, our carelessness. Our dreadfully pathetic selfishness. I hoped one day he'd be able to become happy again.

Tommy was another story. I'd heard (again from Aunty Jane) that Tommy had entered the revolving door of correctional systems after his first initiation into it. Aunty Jane said that Tommy had been back inside, on car theft charges. She wasn't clear on the details, but it seems that the friends Tommy made in his first year in detention became the group he hung with outside of there. And as the old adage goes, when you lie down with dogs, you get fleas. Tommy, it would seem, was teeming with them. I had no sympathy for Tommy. I didn't care about his future, and when I heard his name my lip would curl with derision. It wasn't hard to blame him for everything that had happened. And no, dear reader, I'm not negating my role in the incident, I'd never do that. As I've stated before, it is something I have to live with for the rest of my life. But at night when I was seized with panic that made it hard to breathe I would go over the events in minute detail. If Tommy hadn't recorded what we did, and if the images hadn't gone viral, all we would have had to do was apologise to Annie. I doubt she would ever have forgiven us, and I know we would have wounded her profoundly, but if she hadn't been made the source of such public and extensive ridicule and hate, I believe she would never have tried to end her life. She would never have ended up brain-damaged. I guess some will argue (and I await those comments) that the emotional damage we would have done to her would have been permanent and far-reaching — and maybe that's true. Maybe I am always looking for a way to reduce my guilt. But the way I see it, by posting those photos and video, Tommy turned it into a public spectacle, a reality show that all of us became unwitting participants in. I hated him with a passion I never thought I was capable of.

My counsellor told me the sadness I felt during those exams was grief.

'I don't understand,' I said. 'Annie didn't die. How can it be grief?'

'You all lost something that night,' she said. 'Tommy and Jack lost their freedom, you lost your parents and your self-esteem. And Annie, of course, lost the essence of who she was. You are grieving for her, as if she had died.'

When I heard those words there was no comfort in them. I don't think they were meant to comfort me, really. What my counsellor was doing, as she always did, was put things into a framework I could work through — until I had exhausted all the ramifications. In ways I hadn't realised, I had actually killed a girl.

Post 35: Ghosts from the past

After the meeting with Casey I had to adjust to this realisation. I know from the comments many of you have made on that last post that some see me as highly melodramatic — Annie didn't die, physically. But the girl she once was, the potential of her, we killed. I know now that that's what I've really been grappling with all this time.

And that brings us to the most confrontational day I've faced since, well, Greenheadgate. It was this that led me back to the blog to explain. A bit of a postscript, if you like.

Three weeks ago, I saw him.
It began with Aunty Jane needing a new car —

an eight-seater — to accommodate all the kids and me. We went to a car dealership. She test-drove the latest — it wasn't a sexy car but practical and functional, right — we got to the paperwork and the salesman John went to find the finance guy.

'Back in a sec,' he said as he left the office. Aunty Jane and I sat in the partitioned office chatting about Louie's football results when he put his head through the doorway and said 'Hi'. But that one word chilled my veins and had my head snapping around in a whiplash manoeuvre.

'Hi,' Aunty Jane said. But my own greeting was frozen on my lips. He stood there, impeccably groomed, hair slicked down, holding out his hand. And the most amazing thing happened. I watched his face transform, the persona — the newly cultivated Tommy — slid greasily from his face to the floor, his hand actually went limp and he whispered, 'Jazz?'

A visceral feeling shuddered through me. Tommy. Here. In front of me. Now.

'Tommy,' I croaked, but to my delight it sounded derisive.

'Jazz,' he said again.

'Is there an echo in here?' I asked even more drily.

'Hey,' he said and he slunk into the office and sat behind the desk. Aunty Jane watched this with slight contempt. Of course she knew who he was, she had consoled me over nights I couldn't sleep, when the only name I could utter was Tommy. Oh, trust me, she knew who he was.

'Tommy,' she said assertively, reaching over the desk to offer her hand.

'Hello,' a glimmer of his composure had returned. 'Actually, it's Tom these days.'

'Of *course* it is,' she said, and I smiled internally — there was nothing better she could have said. He was so flummoxed by our presence. He kept writing things down, then scrawling over them and rewriting. 'Sorry,' he said eventually, looking up and wiping sweat off his upper lip, his hand ruffling his hair. 'I need to get a new form. Back in a sec.' He walked self-consciously from the room. Aunty Jane smiled at me.

'He seems a bit out of sorts. How are you?'

'Strange,' I said. Because I hadn't laid eyes on him for so long, I'd kind of caricatured his appearance. In my mind he had black demon eyes and no heart. But this version of him looked like a nervous and anxious boy. It was bizarre. Besides, the last I'd heard he was a dero on his way to an overdose. But no, here he was, working in finance at a car dealership — how did that happen? When he came back it was obvious he'd washed his face; his hair was slicked back down, wet. He put the new form on the table and apologised.

'Mrs Lovely, I'm sorry for my awkwardness earlier. I pride myself on my professionalism, but let's not pretend that this encounter is not, perhaps, unsettling.' I found myself nodding — he sounded all grown up and like a politician. 'I'm hoping, Jazz,' and here he made eye contact and held my gaze firmly, 'that after we've finished here, you and I might be able to catch up with a coffee.' Again I found myself nodding. The idea of sitting down with Tommy was unnerving, to say the least, but it was that same compulsion you have when you pass a car accident and can't look away. Partly you look to see if it's someone you know, and whether or not they're alive. That's exactly the compulsion I felt. Do I know this guy? And is he really alive?

Talk about awkward! It was extreme. Tommy ordered and paid for the coffee, refusing my ten with a quick shake of his head. I sat there silently as we waited for the coffee. I couldn't look at him, yet I was totally aware of him. Where he was, what he was doing. And it was so weird. I wanted to know everything. What had been going on in his life — how he was here, now, with a respectable career and looking like everything was tickety-boo, when last I'd heard he was in the gutter, smoking himself to death. What had happened? The coffee was a welcome distraction from the tension. I stirred mine vigorously as Tommy added sachets of sugar into his. Screwing up the third he laughed lightly, 'Always replace one addiction with another,' he said, 'and you're guaranteed success at quitting the first one.'

'But what about the second one?' I asked involuntarily.

He shrugged. 'Replace it with something else, more benign. Until what you've replaced it with is something normal and functional in society.'

'Like sugar?' I asked.

'Better than ice,' he said. 'I have to watch the

sugar — diabetes, etcetera — but it's a lot less to worry about than meth.'

'Why?' I blurted finally.

'Why sugar over ice? Or why — what — everything?'

'Everything,' I mumbled, 'but start with the ice.'

'Sure,' he shrugged and sipped his coffee. I was too scared to pick mine up, my hands were shaking so hard. 'When I was in Juvenile everything changed. It was hard, Jazz — and I'm not looking for sympathy — but it was so fucking hard. I had no idea. I thought I was tough. Some king shit who could do what he liked — walk over anyone, just do whatever the fuck I wanted. But in there I was nobody. Nothing. They were bigger and stronger and meaner than me. Some of them were evil.'

I couldn't help myself. 'You were evil, Tommy. What you did was evil.'

'No,' he shook his head. 'I wasn't evil. I was fucking stupid. I was nasty. I was mean — but I wasn't evil. I didn't do that shit for Annie to kill herself. I did it because it made me feel important. I wasn't evil. I was just a fucking mean bastard.' He paused and stared into his coffee. 'But I saw evil. There was a guy in there who would slit your throat for nothing. Just because he wanted to. Because he could. I was so scared. It was easy to get into the homemade shit they were cooking up — an easy escape. And so when I finally came out, I was a junkie. And I hadn't finished school. I didn't have a job. I had a record as a sex offender. I'd steal cars, break into houses, take jewellery, small electronics, whatever, just to flog them and get a hit. I went back inside — but this time I was in the real prison — and that evil bastard from Juvenile? He was chicken feed compared to these guys. The meanest and most evil guys in the state. I knew that if I didn't do something this would be it — my life. I made a decision — get off the shit and use the time to get some certificates and qualifications. So I did.'

I didn't want to congratulate him. His little road-to-redemption story. He had dragged us all down and we were all still struggling along. His success seemed unfair.

'Mum picked me up from prison. The whole time I was in, she visited me. Encouraged me, helped me achieve everything I wanted to. Her brother helped get me the job at the dealership, and I'm making good money, I'm clean and working towards real goals.' He sat back and looked at me. I didn't know what to say. There were so many things to say. But they were spiteful. Vitriolic. He was appearing like this Zen Buddha and I was going to go all psycho-crazy on his arse? I didn't speak but stared stonily into my coffee.

'So,' he said eventually, 'the why to everything?' I couldn't look at him. This was it. It was the moment. Why had he done it? 'I guess I've got no real explanation.'

I sighed loudly. Seriously?

'Well, nothing that sounds reasonable. There is no reason, other than what I just told you. I was a mean and nasty person. I was so angry. I blamed Mum for driving Dad away. It was easy to hate her, she was always on at me, all the time. I didn't realise then that it was only because she loved me and wanted the best for me. I was in a state of rage. I hated everyone. I didn't care about who got hurt. I just wanted respect.'

I looked up sharply. 'Respect?' I spat. 'How do you figure abusing, exploiting and raping girls is going to get you respect?'

'It was fucked up,' Tommy agreed. 'Even now,

when I think back to the pictures of Casey, I just wanted to humiliate her — like *I* felt all the time. I was a nasty piece of work — I hated everyone. Women the most.'

'But what you did to Annie ...' I shook my head. That wasn't misogyny — that was criminal.

'I didn't think it was rape,' he said, and held his hand up when he saw my curled lip. 'I know it sounds like bullshit, but I didn't. That word never occurred to me. She was drunk and she deserved it. She led me on. She was a cocktease. It wasn't like she hadn't promised a whole pile of shit before she passed out. And then when she was out, it was like, you said it was okay — so I'll do it.'

'That's disgusting,' I said.

'I know that now,' Tommy said. 'Look, Jazz, I'm not trying to get forgiveness here, I just need to explain, and I need you to know that I'm not that person anymore.'

I don't give a shit, I thought. But why was I still here? What did I want from him?

He continued: 'I would never have sent those photos — or the video — if I'd thought I'd committed a crime. You knew me, I wasn't a total moron. I wouldn't have knowingly incriminated myself — got charges and time — if I'd really thought it was rape.'

'So why?' I was still totally confused.

'To show everyone what a hero I was,' Tommy said, 'to show that I could get with whatever chick I wanted. I wanted their respect, the other guys.' He shook his head. 'I was a total fuckhead.' I nodded in agreement. 'I know you won't forgive me for what I did. I got us in so much trouble.'

'Trouble?' I said. 'You ruined lives, Tommy.'

He dropped his head. 'I know.' When he looked up he had tears in his eyes. 'I ruined Annie's life and Jack's and yours. I know.' He was right — I wasn't going to give him my forgiveness. How could I? Annie was a portion of the person she should have been, Jack — well, there was another story — and as for me, I couldn't forgive myself for the part I'd played, so how was I ever going to forgive him? We were drunk, we were young, we were totally stupid, agreed, but it was still unforgivable. I guess some things just are.

'I've got a girlfriend,' Tommy went on. 'Ciara. She knows about what I did — where I've been. She knows who I am now. I got lucky.'

I could feel myself nodding again. 'You did,' I agreed. 'You got luckier than most of us.'

Later that night, when I couldn't sleep, I thought about his words. 'I got lucky.' It was so unfair, that out of all of us Tommy seemed to have come out of it best. He didn't seem racked by guilt, like I was, when a day couldn't go by that I didn't hate myself. He wasn't mentally altered, like Annie, living in a perpetual childhood, for the rest of his life. And he'd escaped far more lightly than Jack. Jack. Just thinking about it all — my red-haired Jacky Boy, who had held my hand and had always had my back — made me cry again. Jack had suffered far worse than either Tommy or me.

Post 36: Fates worse than death

After seeing Casey and learning about Annie and
then running into Tommy, Greenhead was in my
prefrontal cortex. Everything had come back, with a
vengeance. Frank supported me in talking through
most of it. I still saw Karan, but once a month — not
anywhere near the frequency I used to. It was
Jack. I couldn't forget about Jack anymore. Frank
understood, and offered to go with me, but then he
also understood why I needed to do it alone.

I knocked on the front door and waited nervously.
After what seemed like ages I heard footsteps and
some shouting. A figure loomed behind the glass and
the door opened to a heavily bearded, burly man.

'Yes?' he said, sizing me up. I clutched at my

handbag and immediately felt prissy. I glanced around. What the hell had I been thinking? The overgrown lawn, the bags of rubbish spilling out. Behind the man the hallway was strewn with rubbish, pizza boxes, empty beer bottles. Jack's nan had warned me not to go alone. 'It's not a nice place,' she'd said tearily over the phone. 'His roommates are not very nice.'

I'd had a burning need to see Jack, before it was too late. I was already feeling the fear that I had abandoned him, like I had Annie. Now a part of me wished I'd brought Frank with me. 'Is Jack here?' I asked, finally finding the courage to speak.

'What's ya name?' the man asked.

'Jazz,' I said.

'Wait here,' he pushed the door shut in my face.

I waited, it seemed for hours, but it was probably only ten minutes. I couldn't believe this was it — this was where Jack had ended up. I had Aunty Jane, Uncle Rob, the kids and Frank, Annie had her family, Tommy had a girlfriend and a good job and it was Jack who was living in absolute squalor. Back in Greenhead I would never have believed in a million years that this would have been Jack's future. Never.

The door opened again and despite having prepared myself, I wasn't really prepared. I knew it was Jack, but he looked so old. So worn and lined, with a straggly goatee and filthy old clothes, and while his arms and legs were scrawny, he had a round belly pushing against his t-shirt.

'Hi,' I said, but I couldn't step forward. His eyes narrowed.

'What do you want, Jazz?' he asked.

'I don't know,' I said. 'I wanted to see you. See how you are.'

'Well,' Jack opened the door wider. 'Welcome to my home then. Care to come in?'

The last thing I wanted to do was walk down that filthy hallway, but I had come here to see him. I followed him into the gloom and we walked through a filthy kitchen to a sleep-out on the back verandah.

'Make yourself at home,' Jack said, sweeping a pile of clothes onto the floor. I perched on the edge of his bed. The foam mattress was sheetless and ripped and stained. 'It's not the Taj Mahal,' Jack said, putting a cigarette between his teeth. His beautiful, straight white teeth were varying shades of yellow and one of his eyeteeth was snapped off. He lit the cigarette and drew in a huge lungful. 'What's new with you?'

'I start uni in a couple of months,' I began, but the minute the words left my mouth I regretted them. I sounded boastful and proud and totally disregarding of Jack's situation.

'Oh yeah,' Jack scratched his arm where a faded blue tattoo curled over his forearm — it looked like a homemade job. 'Whatcha studying?'

'Psychology,' I said. He laughed loudly, and for a second I had gone back in time with the sound of Jack's laughter.

'You know what they say,' he said, 'those who study psych only do it to figure out their own shit.'

I nodded. Of course it was true. I was fascinated by behaviours, why people made the choices they did despite knowing it was a bad idea. I laughed too. 'How else do you think I'm ever going to figure out my family?'

'Yeah,' Jack scratched again. 'Heard from them? How's your dad?'

'Nah.' I said it lightly, as though it didn't bother me, but since the day of the court case I hadn't laid eyes on either one of them. Aunty Jane kept me updated — she was in phone contact with my mum — and lately Mum had been making murmurings that she'd like to visit me. But I wasn't sure. It was like I didn't even exist to them anymore — they had wiped me away when I needed family the most. As for Dad, the last contact I'd had with him had been my day in court. It was like he'd disappeared. Or never existed. And I had a sense of loyalty to Aunty Jane and Uncle Rob, despite both of them (and Frank too) saying it was okay to reacquaint with my parents. 'They're on a cruise. You?'

'Yeah.' Jack shook his head. 'Mum and Dad both been round. Asking me to come home. Like I even have a home. Can't go back to Greenhead. Blew it at Nan's. This is it, this is where guys like me end up.' He scratched even harder at his arm. 'Fucken scabies.'

'What happened at your nan's?' I looked at his arm, razed with tiny red marks, some weeping and irritated. I was pretty sure scabies was highly infectious. I wriggled uncomfortably on the bed.

'She reckons I took money,' Jack looked away. 'She didn't believe me. Said it was me or me mates. Things got a bit heated.'

'What did you do?' I almost whispered. Jack

shrugged and looked at me from under his brows. I knew that look. It meant he was about to lie.

'Nothin', it was an accident. I put my hand up and accidently hit her. She fell and broke her hip. After that she had to go to hospital and Uncle Mick told me I had to get out. Like I done it on purpose. It was bullshit.'

'Is she alright?' She hadn't mentioned it to me when I'd spoken to her. She'd said the broken hip was because of a fall, but didn't mention Jack. He was still being protected by people who loved him.

'Yeah,' Jack shrugged, 'she'll be fine.' We sat in awkward silence for a while. I wanted to study Jack, but I didn't want him to see me watching him. I glanced at him several times, but he was more interested in his cigarette and scratching his tattoo than making small talk. It was palpable — the strangeness between us. 'So,' he said finally, 'I gotta get going. Work.'

'Oh,' I gathered up my bag. I don't know why but I'd assumed he was unemployed. 'What do you do?'

He lifted an eyebrow at me. 'Really, Jazz?'

I shook my head, perplexed. What was so obvious? He lived in squalor, his teeth were rotting, his clothes filthy — what could anyone do for work and still not have any money?

'Put it this way, it's a supply and demand industry,' he smiled, showing me that broken tooth again. 'It's not going to make me rich, but at least I'm not on the streets yet.'

He walked behind me to the door.

'Nice to see you, Jack,' I said awkwardly. Shake hands? Hug? I didn't know what to do. I ended up going to pat his shoulder but instead patted his elbow. It looked and felt weird.

'Yeah,' Jack said, beginning to shut the door.

I walked down the steps and he called out my name. The door was almost shut. 'Why didn't you come back?'

He pulled on my heart, plaintive Jack, ten-year-old Jack who I'd left at the park in anger once and two hours later, after waiting patiently for me, believing I'd return, he'd come to my house to ask me that very same question. 'Why didn't you come back?'

I shook my head and swallowed the tears. 'I don't know,' I said. 'I'm sorry.'

'I'm sorry too,' he said, closing the door.

Post 37: Time moves on and takes no prisoners

Dear reader, you'll notice that since re-engaging with this blog I've taken to weekly updates. I've fallen back into the social purge — airing one's innermost thoughts and actions online. It's a long way from Facebook, but it's a similar psychology.

I think about Jack often. I've started talking about him more and more. Frank wants to know about the friendship we shared, and he's commented that such a strong relationship like the one Jack and I had doesn't just end. But, unusually, I disagree with Frank. It has ended. It can no longer be the same, or even a semblance of what it was, because we are so different. And I don't mean because I'm about to study at university and Jack is a small-time drug dealer — it's greater than that. We have changed, shaped by a single night, into people we didn't see ourselves becoming. I am closer to the person I always thought I'd be, and for the most part I'm happy. Who wouldn't be, with Frank at their side and family (by this I mean Uncle Rob, Aunty Jane and the bratpack) supporting them? But I still get dragged back into that world, where everything went pear-shaped for me. Frank tells me part of my beauty is this fragility I acquired.

'You can look at it as the worst thing you've ever experienced and regret it for the rest of your life, or you can acknowledge it's the worst thing you've ever experienced and it's allowed you to develop into a unique, passionate and empathetic person.' Oh Frank, always seeing the best of me.

But you know what? He's right. Without that experience I wouldn't be half of who I am today. I hadn't realised I'd lived a loveless life until I met Aunty Jane and Uncle Rob — and, of course, Frank. Between them they've given me so much — so much I didn't even know I was missing. So when I think about the horrors of that night I wind it back into perspective. I allow myself to acknowledge that life is beautiful and there are so many things to look forward to.

Soon, I'll be starting university. I don't know what to expect. I've been out of formal education for so long that the idea of sitting in a classroom sends my anxiety into overdrive. I can only imagine that it'll be different to high school. Older people, wiser people who hopefully, like me, have made their colossal mistakes and now just want to move forward. It's hard to imagine that high school bitchiness will carry over into tertiary education. But anyway, I've learnt from my errors — the power of social media — and I won't be venturing down that track again. As a devotee of blogs I'm totally aware of the differences between the two platforms — and the power this one allows me. I get time. Time to think about what I want to say. Time to consider the ramifications of every word I post for the world to read. Instead of firing off some random comment, or image, that can cause ripples, resulting in a tsunami, I get to consider what I do.

It's funny, though, how people view me when I say I don't have a Facebook account. It's like I'm an alien — or from a different culture. 'You don't have

Facebook?' The tone is always incredulous. I shake my head.

'I prefer real people,' I say, 'not phantoms.'

Post 38: A new bully

Another lapse in communication — my apologies.
I started uni a few months back and I have found
myself immersed in the most wonderful world
imaginable. Uni houses the most eclectic group
of people I've ever met. Students from around the
world, of differing religions and political convictions.
I feel as though I have actually finally entered the
real world. Teachers, or should I say lecturers, are
human beings — with views and opinions and many
swear words littering their conversations. I think
I've been waiting for this my whole life. Up until
now, everything has been like learning scales, but
now I'm actually playing in the orchestra.

It's exhilarating and thrilling. My life is so busy
— but now I know why busy is good. And I love

study! It's bizarre. Before, study was about getting good marks, making my parents proud, proving how clever I was (remember 'She might be pretty but she's as thick as pig shit'?). Now it's about learning and understanding the world I live in and the people in it. I love it. Every day I walk past the inscription on the wall of the Arts building, *Know Thyself*, and now I really understand. To know thyself would have to be the greatest knowledge of all.

But nothing is ever smooth sailing. Yes, things are wonderful, but there are always tests and challenges. My fear of high school bitchiness was not totally unfounded, but it is coming from an unexpected source. I do a unit in my degree called Psychology and Social Behaviour — sounds exceptionally boring, but it's not. It examines the factors that influence the way we think and behave in social situations. It allows me to examine my own values and attitudes to life. I'm learning so much in this class. But despite loving it, I fear I've run foul of the lecturer. His name is Earl Stirling and of all my lecturers he is the best, the most engaging. He's a short balding man, and wears tight jeans that hug every (and yes I mean every!) curve on his body. He tops them with a muscle t-shirt, and for someone who must be closer to sixty than fifty, he sports a couple of guns. He wears his thinning hair in a sort of comb-over — which deludes no one, as most people are a good six inches taller than him — and what he lacks in height he overcompensates for with the loudest booming voice imaginable. Where some three-hour lectures have me drawing flowers all over my notebook, Earl's are the ones where I remain fully focused. So I was thrilled when I landed Earl for the small-group tutorials.

Thirteen of us cram into a six-person seminar room. We sit, knees touching, as we examine the weekly topic. It was at the first of these when I guess I captured Earl's attention.

'Oh look,' Earl said, peering at me through his bifocals, 'we've got ourselves a Teen Queen.'

I realised he was talking about me. A few of the girls snickered and I began to feel embarrassed.

'Me?' I asked. 'What do you mean?'

'You don't fit the mould of a uni student,' Earl said, eyeing me up and down. I still wasn't sure what he meant, but then I assessed my appearance. Unlike most of my counterparts I had dressed nicely for class. Many looked like they'd slept in their clothes, but I wore neat, fashionable ones, I'd done my hair, I wore make-up. I didn't know what to say. But it was Maureen, the mature-aged student, who responded.

'I think she looks lovely,' she said to Earl in clipped tones. 'And I think it's inappropriate for a man in your position to make such a comment.'

Talk about awkward. The rest of us shifted uneasily and I smiled gratefully at Maureen while Earl glowered at her.

'Right,' he said opening the textbook, 'page ninety-four.'

It probably wouldn't warrant writing about if it had ended there, but it hasn't. I'm afraid Earl has truly shaken my self-confidence. Today I met with him to receive my first marked assignment. Since the first tutorial, Earl had pretty much ignored me, but today it was face-to-face, alone in his office. I sat opposite him. I was pretty sure I'd done well on this topic. Essay writing had always been my forte and I'd ended up in the nineties for Literature at the end of last year, so I wasn't overly concerned about getting the assignment back. He sort of threw it across the table. I picked it up and on my neatly typed work he had scrawled over every paragraph in illegible writing. I peered at his words — the characters were drawn with such force I could only assume reading my words had enraged him somehow. I struggled over each page, my confidence diminishing with each scrawled-out word and margin comment. Then I turned to the back page: twelve out of twenty-five. I looked at the digits in disbelief. I had failed. My first assignment, failed.

'Oh,' was all I could manage.

'The brevity of your response surprises me,' Earl said nastily. 'With such laborious and verbose sentences, rife with tautology, I must admit, Miss Lovely, I was expecting a lot more than *oh*.'

I shook my head, my mouth dry. 'I'm sorry, I wasn't expecting this.'

'Well, surely you weren't expecting to pass?' Earl said. 'Girl, you are verging on illiterate. All I can think is that the once lofty standards of this institution have dropped markedly to allow someone of your calibre in.' His voice was softer than the booming lecturer, but his comments were so snide that I felt stupid. I started to feel that I had no place whatsoever at this uni. I felt tears in my eyes.

'Oh for God's sake don't cry,' Earl snapped, pointing to a box of tissues (which made me wonder if they were on his desk solely for this reason). 'You need additional help. Hopefully it'll be enough to get you over the line. You need to meet with me weekly, for private tuition, if you want any chance of passing. So,' he looked at his calendar, 'we'll start next Thursday.'

I was too mortified to speak. I felt the old, scared Jasmine creeping back in. *Fight her off*, I told myself. I wasn't going to let the old patterns of thinking in. I liked the new me so much better. *Toughen up*, I told myself, and to Earl I said, 'Thank you. I'll see you then.' I decided immediately that I wouldn't allow myself to fail this unit and I wouldn't be a crybaby over it. I needed to learn resilience. I'd meet with Earl weekly to improve my marks and reach my goals.

Post 39: What is sexual harassment?

So it's been two months since I last posted and I'm pleased to say my results (with the exception of Psychology and Social Behaviour) have all been distinctions and high distinctions. I still love uni, walking along the footpaths, listening to the squawk of the peacocks as they strut around fanning their tails, overhearing the debates in the coffee shop and inhaling the distinctive smell of the library. It's addictive. I keep looking at my units and where I'm heading. I have no real fixed plan but to keep learning, and I have my weekly tutes and my weekly private tutes with Earl still. He believes that I have to continue this extra tuition until the end of the year.

One day I was in the Reid Library, asking the

library attendant where I would find a particular book to help with my latest assignment, when my phone vibrated in my pocket. I looked at the number and frowned — I didn't know it. I tapped on the message.

> **Teen Queen. You need to go to High Demand and stop wasting time posing around the library. The information you need is in the book I marked on your tute notes. Earl.**

I may have gasped when I saw it and looked around the library suspiciously, anticipating I'd see Earl peering at me between the bookshelves. The library attendant looked up from the computer. 'It's listed in High Demand,' he said, nodding in that direction.

'Thanks,' I said, stuffing my phone back in my pocket. 'Yeah, stupid, I should have read my course papers better.'

'Oh not really,' the library attendant said, 'it was only listed there this morning. Understandable mistake.'

I was fuming as I headed for High Demand and pushed the glass door open. I'd spent the better part of the morning looking for that stupid book. If Earl was going to list it High Demand — when the only person in the course it was relevant to was me — why wouldn't he have told me earlier? Seriously, I think he got off on making my life difficult.

It was only much later that it occurred to me that he had somehow accessed my mobile number, so I made him a contact in my phone — that way I wouldn't be caught off guard by him again.

Not long after this, Maureen, the mature-aged student, was enraged after our tute. She grabbed hold of my arm and whispered, 'I'm going to complain about him.' I was puzzled. In group tutorial Earl pretty much ignored me now, whereas in our private sessions he was totally different, belittling me, reminding me how dumb and superficial I was. So I wasn't sure what had Maureen so mad.

'Why?' I asked.

'I hate the way he speaks to you,' she said. 'I can't stand it. I have a daughter your age and if I thought any man spoke to her the way Earl does to you I'd want someone to stand up for her.'

'Oh Maureen,' I said. She didn't know the half of

his treatment towards me. 'It's fine, really.'

'It's not,' Maureen hissed. 'It's an abuse of power. He cuts you down, his tone is rude. He doesn't speak to anyone else the way he speaks to you.' I had to agree it was true, but at least he wasn't making public the nasty comments he made to me privately. 'It's akin to sexual harassment.'

Sexual harassment? I wanted to laugh. There was nothing sexual coming from him. He certainly had never made any moves on me — that, I'd have reported in a heartbeat. No, he was just a mean old man, who had made me his target.

'Please don't,' I said. 'Really, I can handle it. I think that's why he does it. It's just a bit of banter.'

Maureen looked unconvinced but warned me that if she thought he was overstepping the mark again she'd be complaining, with or without my permission.

The following week I walked up to Earl's office for our session. He was standing just outside his office, talking to a guy about my age.

'Go in, Jasmine,' Earl said, nodding towards the door. 'I'll be in with you in a minute.' As I walked in I heard Earl say to the guy, 'I should introduce you to Jasmine, but I'm not really sure how many sexually transmitted diseases she has.'

I turned sharply. Earl was closing the door with a smug look on his face.

'What did you say that for?' I asked. I was shocked. Had he really said that? Had I misheard him? Surely no professor would make a comment of that nature about a student to another student?

He laughed. 'It's just a joke, me and Jonah make jokes like that all the time.'

'It's not funny.' I was close to tears. The mean things Earl had said to me over the last few months had always been about my intelligence (or lack of), not about my sexuality.

'Toughen up, Teen Queen,' Earl said. 'Come on, we don't have time to waste if we want that pretty little head to absorb information into that piece of cement you call a brain.'

Lately he's taken to sending me messages via the university email system. At least twice a week there would be a reminder from him about something I needed to do before the next lecture, or tute, or 'special' tute. Most of the messages were generic to the class, but he'd always add a personal touch to mine. Signing off with: *Don't be distracted by other interests, Teen Queen.* Or: *Think before you act and are late to class.* Nothing overtly nasty, but because I can hear his voice and tone, see his snide smile, his messages just make me feel stupid and reinforce the idea that I don't belong at the university.

It's all so confusing. Maureen's words are still in my ears — is this really sexual harassment? Or is he just a bored old professor looking for a landing spot for his meanness? Is he like Tommy — a nasty piece of work? Or is he really some sort of sexual predator? And who would I talk to anyway? And what could I say — Earl is being mean to me?

When I put it into this perspective, it seems trivial. And again I acknowledge those of you who have drawn parallels between Earl's behaviour (bullying has been mentioned many times) and the things said to Annie. And I agree with many of you — Annie endured far worse than just some random insults from a geriatric academic. That helps keep things in perspective for me.

Post 40: Contact

The effects of Greenheadgate continue to ripple through our lives. Sometimes I wonder if we'll ever be free of that night. And I know I am making enormous progress, I know I've managed to carve out a shiny future – even with its bumps – but every now and again a reminder of that night pops up. Today was one of the worst ones ever.

I was sitting down for a break at Chicco this morning. Frank dropped the newspaper over my shoulder and bent down to kiss my ear as I looked straight into Jack's eyes. I gasped.

'What?' Frank said, by my side in an instant. 'What is it? You've gone white.'

'Jack,' I said and pointed to the front page of the paper. It was a half-page picture of Jack handcuffed and being led towards a van. The headline above it said: LOCAL MAN ARRESTED FOR DRUG TRAFFICKING IN BALI.

'Oh my God,' I read the article to Frank. 'Australian officials confirm that three Australian men were arrested at Denpasar airport attempting to smuggle nine-and-a-half kilograms of heroin out of Indonesia. The three are being detained at Kerobokan prison awaiting trial. If found guilty they will face execution by firing squad under Indonesia's tough penalties for drug trafficking.' I looked at Frank. 'Oh God.'

'Oh God,' Frank echoed. 'What do you want to do?'

'What can I do?' I asked, emotions hitting me forcefully. 'I haven't spoken to him since last year and I don't even have his mother's contact details. Oh, Maria will be beside herself.'

'Who would know how to get in touch with her? Is that what you want to do?' Frank asked.

'I think I need to talk to her,' I nodded. 'I guess the only person who'll know her number is my mum.'

The phone rang out and then went to voicemail. Listening to my dad's clipped words brought a whole pile of memories, and not all of them bad, into my head. I left what I hoped was an airy and cheerful message.

'Hi, it's Jasmine. I've just seen the paper and Jack is in trouble. I wanted to speak to Maria but I don't have her number. Mum, could you call me back please?' I tapped the hang-up icon and looked at Aunty Jane.

'How do you feel?' she asked.

'Weird,' I said. 'Just hearing Dad's voice made me feel strange, like that song, "Now you're just somebody that I used to know". And I'm nervous about speaking to Mum too,' I shrugged. 'Poor Jack.'

'It's so awful,' Aunty Jane said, 'he got totally fucked up.'

'Yeah,' I bit my lip, 'it makes me realise how lucky I got when you came and rescued me.' These days we don't really talk about Greenhead, or my life before I came to live with them. But this new incident, of course, brought it all back.

'It seems like a lifetime ago,' Aunty Jane said.

'It's been over three years,' I said.

'I can't remember a time when you weren't part of this family,' Aunty Jane said wistfully.

'Me neither,' I agreed. 'It's like that other Jasmine, the one who lived in Greenhead and did those terrible things, well, it's like she was something I invented — a dream, and this is the real me.'

Aunty Jane smiled. 'That's because this *is* the real you.' The phone rang and I looked at Aunty Jane almost fearfully.

'Shall I answer it for you?' Aunty Jane asked.

'No,' I shook my head, 'I'll do it.' I picked up my phone.

'Hi,' I said and heard my mother's voice, 'Hi Mum.'

We talked for about forty minutes. She asked all sorts of questions that I knew she had the answers to. Aunty Jane had made no secret of the fact that over the years she had kept up a regular phone relationship with Mum. I sensed Mum just wanted to hear about it from me. When the call was almost ending and she'd given me Maria's number, she said, 'Jasmine, I'm so proud of you.'

I was taken aback. My mother — proud of me? The desire to please her and Dad had long gone, replaced by a desire to please those in my family who had been there for me. Still, it made my voice thicken.

'Thank you,' I said eventually.

'I'm so proud of how you've turned your life around. Sometimes I wish I'd done things differently.' I heard tears in her own voice — my mother the Iron Lady was crying? Time and distance can do surprising things to people.

'It's okay,' I said, realising I meant it. If they hadn't turned their backs on me (no matter how much it still hurt) I'd never have got to this point in my life. I had the perspective, now I needed to use it. We hung up, after she'd asked if it would be okay to call me every other week. I said it would be. I wasn't sure if we would have much to talk about, but I figured it was worth a shot.

Post 41: No boundaries

Again, apologies for my absence, but things got really busy in my part of the world. Particularly juggling uni exams, work and socialising, so sitting down pouring my heart out is not something I've prioritised. But given recent events, I thought you might like to know how things went with my mate Earl.

I kept to my weekly sessions with him, and there was nothing major to report (apart from his usual snide comments in person and by text and email) except three separate incidents.

The first started outside of his room (which in itself was unusual). I was in the library coffee shop, working on my latest assignment for him, when he pulled out a chair and sat down.

'Make yourself comfortable,' I said dismissively,

not looking up. I knew it was him from his cheap aftershave and the tight denim in my peripheral vision. As you can gather, I now spoke to him as rudely as he spoke to me.

'I want you to give me a lift to uni tomorrow. I'm putting my car in for a service,' he said. I nearly choked on my raspberry liquorice.

'What?' I said, looking at him and frowning. 'No way. No. Anyway I don't know where you live. It might be miles out of my way.'

'It's not. I've looked you up on the university records,' he said smugly. 'I live in Menora, right next door.'

I shook my head. 'No way.' The idea of being alone with him in a car made me feel sick.

'I don't think that's a nice response,' he said sternly. 'After all the extra time I've put in for you, I'd think you'd want to help me out. Quid pro quo.'

I sighed. He did put in extra time, even if it was his perverted way of making me miserable. Suddenly it occurred to me that it might be a very bad idea to turn him down. 'Okay,' I agreed, 'what's the address?'

Frank thought it was weird. 'Surely he has work

mates that could give him a lift. What professor asks a student?'

Frank didn't know about the shit Earl said to me, because I was being resilient (so I thought), so I brushed off his concerns. 'He gives me lots of help, seems okay.'

'If you think so,' Frank said finally, 'but I don't think it's right. And looking up a student's personal details seems like a total abuse of power.'

When I picked Earl up that morning from his pokey little cottage he was buoyant and chirpy. He had a real spring in his step as he got into the front of my car. 'Okay, Teen Queen, I hope your driving skills are better than your writing skills.'

Inwardly I groaned, but as it wasn't far to uni, I knew I wouldn't have to endure him for too long.

It was long enough. He criticised my driving, even feigning alarm that I wasn't allowing enough room for braking. 'Good lord, girl,' he said, taking his feet down off the dash where he had put them in a mock brace position, 'how did you get your licence? By smiling sweetly at the examiner, no doubt.'

I gritted my teeth. When I arrived at uni I felt emotionally wrecked. By the time I was in my

second lecture my nerves were less jangly, but
then my phone vibrated. Earl's name, text message.
Every time I saw his name appear on my phone I'd
hold my breath, waiting to see what this message
heralded. This time he didn't disappoint. He'd
sent a photo. It was of me, with Annie and Jack,
at Casey's birthday back in the summer holidays
before Year 10. I reeled at the image. It was weeks
before Greenheadgate. Two people I hadn't seen
for so long. Two people who at that time had meant
the world to me. Two people who were now both
effectively dead. Everything came crashing back
down on me. Everything I'd been through, and tried
to recover from. And suddenly, in an instant, with
one picture, I was right back there. In Greenhead.
The lecturer was warbling on, but I had to get out.

I gathered up my laptop and stumbled up
the stairs, wheezy and panicked. Outside in the
fresh air the other realisation hit me. Where had
Earl got this picture from? I studied it again — it
was a screenshot, from somebody in Greenhead's
Facebook page. I shook my head. How bored was
the man? That when he looked up my records
he also googled me? Stalker much? Thank God

my real name was never tagged to this blog. Yet when I really thought about his obvious physical disinterest in me, I started to feel melodramatic. This wasn't really stalking, or even sexual harassment, I thought. It was just Earl thinking he would get a rise out of me. I wasn't special, it was just really nothing. And when I put it into that perspective, that he'd never tried to hit on me, never tried anything of a sexual nature with me like asking me out or getting physical, then I had to accept that the man just had poor — really, totally, poor — social skills.

After the initial shock wore off I knew I wouldn't even give him the pleasure of confronting him. That was what he wanted from me, some reaction, and then he could patronise me and belittle me. I wouldn't give him the opportunity. And had he remained a harmless dick, then I might have been okay.

But that's not where this tale with Earl ends, dear reader. There's more.

A few weeks passed and then I had another of my weekly sessions with Earl. We were heading into exams and Earl was really hitting me with pressure that I wasn't good enough and not even he, the wondrous Professor Stirling, could teach krill how to think.

'When I look at your fluency,' he said rifling the papers in front of him, 'I'm surprised you can even string two sentences together. It's disjointed and awkward. Incorrect use of preposition,' he struck through my paragraph with his stubby lead pencil. I considered that the pencil was a miniature replica of him. Short and ugly, used to shout obscenities at me, like his great booming voice. I had toughened myself against him. I viewed him detachedly. He was huffing and puffing over my massacre of English and he was really stupid to watch. He was getting all worked up over parts of speech and I couldn't have cared less. He was boring me, pontificating over my syntax and vocabulary, and I looked out the window at Winthrop Hall. It's such a magnificent tower, and I sat there thinking about the day I'll eventually graduate, walk up the stairs into the hall and receive my degree. It seemed magical and somewhat elusive.

'Teen Queen, can you hear me?' I was brought back to reality.

'Sorry, I drifted off,' I said automatically. Well, how to load Earl's gun and point it at me. I watched him inhale.

'That's what makes it so challenging to teach someone like you. The amount of air inside that head would cause anything to drift off. It must be like a tornado in there, hurtling ideas around and around.' He was obviously pleased with this clever analogy as he elaborated on it for another minute. Frankly, I was fed up with his petty abuse, so I interrupted him by pointing to the tower. 'That's where students graduate,' I stated.

'Yes, students do,' Earl said, 'but, Jasmine, it's unlikely you'll ever get the opportunity at the rate you're going.'

I shrugged. His arrows weren't even pointy anymore.

'What's the view like from the top?' I asked.

He shook his head. 'You can't get up there, it's blocked off.'

'Why?' I asked.

'Suicide,' Earl said. I shuddered and looked at the tower. If you jumped from there no one would be able to put you back together.

'Students from Psychology and Social Behaviour 101, no doubt,' I quipped. His face changed, went grey and slightly saggy.

'Don't even joke about it,' he said grimly.

The weird atmosphere was disturbed, thankfully, by the ringing phone. Earl lifted the receiver and started speaking. I sat there twiddling a pen, thinking about what I was going to wear to Frank's gig and everything that had nothing to do with this course. I looked around the room, stuffed to the ceiling with books, and not just on psychology — on poetry, art, history. I noticed fiction in there too. Earl was obviously intelligent, well read, highly educated. He was a brilliant lecturer. So why did he feel the need to be so awful to me? What had I done to offend him? My clothing, my appearance?

'No, I've got Jasmine here.' I looked over at the mention of my name. 'Yes, she's a first-year student who's really thick. Needs all the help she can get. Hang on, I'll put her on.' He waved the phone at me. I shook my head, I wasn't playing his ridiculous games. He shoved the phone into my hand. I sighed.

'Hello,' I said. The voice on the other end belonged to a man.

'Is Earl giving you a hard time?' he asked.

'Earl always gives me a hard time,' I replied. 'He's a right wanker.' Within the ten months I'd been at uni I'd learned that teacher–student relationships were vastly different to those at school. And while I didn't make a habit of calling my lecturers obscenities, Earl deserved it. Earl, of course, found it funny. He always seemed invigorated if I fought back. He laughed delightedly at my comment, as did the man on the other end. I handed the phone back in disgust. I felt like a toy being used for two little boys' amusement. This was getting weird.

'*What*? Invite *her* to lunch?' Earl said to the other man. I screwed my face up at him. As if! Earl listened, then said, 'Yes, she is as pretty as she sounds, but we don't know how many men she's been through by this time of the day.' My mouth dropped open in sheer shock. Surely he hadn't just said that? It was one (rather disgusting) thing to imply that kind of thing to a student, but to say it to another grown man? Possibly another lecturer at the uni? To make up things about me and spread them around, in front of me? He had gone too far. That was it. I'd had enough.

'Fuck you,' I snarled and walked out the door, slamming it as hard as I could behind me.

I walked out of the building angrily. What an arse. Everything started falling into place. Maureen had been right. This *was* a classic case of sexual harassment, but I hadn't seen it because there had been nothing overtly sexual, until more recently. Earl had cultivated the situation, groomed me into accepting his behaviour and then pushed the boundary that much further away.

I wasn't sure what to do, so I pulled out my phone and called Karan for an appointment.

Post 42: Finding the power

'I just put up with his shit all year,' I said to Karan.
'I didn't tell anyone what was happening. I just
thought I needed to learn resilience.'

'It's interesting that you use that word —
resilience. What do you think it means?' Karan
asked.

'I guess ...' I frowned. What did it actually mean?
'I guess I thought it meant being tough. Not running
to someone every time things got hard. Learning to
stand up for myself.'

'And to a certain extent you're right,' Karan
nodded. 'Often people think bullying or harassment
is when someone makes a random unkind comment
— even a threat. But it's not. It's repeated. Sustained.
Which is what you endured — and for nearly a year.

Is that why you think you kept this to yourself?'
Karan asked.

'I don't know.' I started racking my brain. At
what point had I made the decision to suck it up? 'I
guess it didn't seem that bad, not when I compared it
to Annie.'

'So that was your benchmark? Sexual abuse and
systematic bullying versus sexual harassment from a
lecturer?'

'I didn't even consider it as sexual harassment,
and truthfully if Maureen had never mentioned those
words I'm not sure if it would ever have fallen into
place. He made me feel stupid. I thought I was so
dumb and had no right to be at uni. He embarrassed
me, that's why I really kept it to myself. I didn't want
anyone to know, because what if he was right and
then by telling others they recognised that in me too?'

'You see the power imbalance here?' Karan
asked. I nodded.

'That's when it actually all slotted together,' I
said. 'He had made veiled threats about what was
in my best interests before, and I guess on some
level I was aware of that. He'd texted me and
emailed me — but within the system, so I thought

it was within the boundaries. But it was that incident — where he basically told some guy that I was a slut — that made me see exactly how much power he had. I felt like a plaything, because I was. He's actually a sick and disgusting animal.'

'What do you want to do?' Karan said.

'I don't know,' I said. 'I'm still aware how this could affect my grades, but then that makes me feel angry. Keep my mouth shut, so as not to jeopardise my marks?'

'You don't know how many others he's doing this to. Or whether he'll do it to someone else after you, if he gets away with it,' Karan said. 'And if we look at his behaviour, his comments started escalating, becoming more sexual, entering different forums — text, email, looking up your personal details, finding photos of you — there's no reason to suggest this wasn't the step before physical contact. As you pointed out, he kept shifting the boundaries further out.'

That made up my mind. I had stood by before and done nothing. I had been cowardly when tested. Now I had to confront my fear. I hadn't defended others — but noticeably, I hadn't defended myself. If

I allowed Earl to get away with it, what was I saying about me, Jasmine Lovely? That I wasn't worth protecting? That I didn't deserve basic fundamental human rights? Earl had sent me a photo of my life before Greenheadgate — but if everyone involved hadn't scurried like rats in the light when the police homed in on Greenheadgate, then Earl might easily have found a screenshot of me in that room with Annie. And then what? That whole sordid affair would be front-page news in my new life? *Those pictures will always haunt you*, the cop had said, but the reality was, *her words* actually haunted me. Now I knew I did deserve protecting, so I went to the Student Grievance Officer and lodged a complaint.

When I'd completed the written form I looked at all the times he'd insulted me and the things he'd said, emailed and texted — there were so many. And although each one individually was a minor graze of the ego, or self, collectively they amounted to a tirade of abuse. The grievance officer gave me a small smile. 'You're being very brave,' she said as I left.

Earl was waiting for me as I walked through the doors to sit my final three-hour exam for Psych and

Social Behaviour. It was his final shot. He walked up to me as I sat at my desk, my student number in front of me. He bent down and whispered in my ear, 'I'm glad I saw you, Jasmine. I wanted to wish you the very best of luck. Given your semester average, if you don't make fifty per cent you will fail this course. And I'll make sure you never do another Psychology unit at this institution again.' He walked off without looking at me. I was shaken, but not freaked out. In fact, he gave me strength, because more than anything else I wanted to have psychology as a career option — so I could figure out what made dickheads like him tick.

I never really found out what happened to Earl after my grievance, but I heard whispers that there had been others. I guess if by complaining about him he got removed from the frontline, then that's a victory for all future female students.

Oh, and I might add I got seventy-two for that exam — it was marked externally, so Earl was unable to bring my marks down to the low fifties he always awarded me. It was a great feeling to finally be vindicated, to know that despite everything he'd thrown at me, I'd overcome it.

I'd promised myself years earlier that I'd save myself, and I guess I finally did.

So that leaves me to sign off. This time for good. Life is too busy to spend ruminating over the past, psychoanalysing one's self on a blog site, opening up to a world of strangers and their thoughts and opinions. The cruelty of people is really what started this whole saga, and I have decided I don't need that anymore. It is the opinion of those I love that counts, not some random comment by someone I'll never know. It is also my opinion of me that matters the most. When I started this blog I never thought I'd recover from Greenheadgate. I'm still not convinced I ever will. As you have seen, dear reader, often things happen that drag it all to the surface again. So those images *will* always haunt me, and I'll never forget the part I played. But I'll use my perspective and resilience to keep it where it needs to be — firmly in the past. As a piece of me, that helped form the me I am today. So now, almost four years from where I began, I wish you all the best. So long, farewell, adieu, ciao.

Post 43: The final addendum

My name is Jasmine Lovely, Jazz usually (unless I'm in trouble, and do I try to avoid that), and I'm a clinical psychologist.

When I was sixteen I declared to the world that I was a rapist and spent a long time trying to explain my actions. I haven't visited this blog since I signed off all those years ago, but for my dissertation I was doing research into sexting and when I googled several relevant terms, my own blog came up in the results. Rereading it was like sifting through a shoebox of old photographs. I even felt sorry for that younger Jazz, the girl who maintained she was a rapist and maybe even a murderer, the girl who hated herself so much. It compelled me to write this final post (I was surprised I remembered my password to this account — but of course it was JackyWest, as it always was), to prove to the world that there is nothing we can't overcome.

It has taken seven years of full-time study to get my qualification, and over those years I've been able to examine the behaviours of my parents and my friends, but more importantly, I've been able to understand myself. As we know, my journey of self-discovery began with a horrific drunken escapade, but through it all it got me questioning what underpinned the way I behaved. It became clear that I had some genuine father issues. And I've since identified a lot of patterns of my dad's behaviour in men who seek to control women. I remain estranged from my father. His will was unbending, he could never accept what I'd done, nor any of the efforts I made to rectify it. Trying to please him and regain his acceptance of me was torturous, and it was Karan who told me to let it go. I do see my mother, though. She remains with my father and she knows that I know the truth about him now, so she is a bit more gentle these days. Her primness was her own mechanism for dealing with my father's dominance. 'Walking on eggshells' was what creeping around someone like Dad felt like. It is not a feeling you ever forget.

Now, you might like to hear about my nemesis Earl Stirling. He was moved slowly, by the university, from lecturing into the sole role of researcher, never to have student contact. My PhD supervisor told me this many years after I'd made my grievance against Earl.

'You know, Jazz, I knew about you when you became my second-year student,' Professor Michael Milton told me. 'I had marked your first paper and I was astounded by the quality of your writing and so I referred to your academic record. When I saw you had only received a very marginal pass for your first-year unit I phoned Earl up and asked him why this potential Honours student had done so badly in first year.'

'What did he say?' I asked.

'He laughed and said, "Oh Mike, don't tell me she's batting her eyelashes at you already?"'

I shook my head. 'It's one thing I never understood — why he despised me so much.'

Mike frowned at me. 'Seriously, Jazz. With all

your understanding of social behaviours you never figured Earl out?'

'No,' I said. 'His scorn was immediate, his hostility visible and his reasoning unhinged. I thought he was bored.'

'He was infatuated,' Mike said. 'Jazz, you weren't the first and until they moved him to no student contact, you weren't the last. Every year he selected a first-year student who was the subject of his attentions. In the Faculty lounge you girls were known as the Stirling Club.'

'They knew about us?' I was horrified.

'There were whispers and rumours about Earl's "special tuition sessions". Earl himself, in later years, made no secret of his "first-year girls" — but aside from some whispered complaints, no girl had ever risked coming forward. Your complaint was the first formal one made. You saved a lot of girls from him that day.'

'But the university keeps him employed,' I said.

'He's a tenured professor. They're hard to get rid of — until the inevitable. So they just moved him out of harm's way.'

'So where is he now?' I asked.

'They gave him an office, up near the top of Winthrop Hall,' Mike said.

Aunty Jane and Uncle Rob finally got the second set of twins, Bernie and Jake, through high school and are awaiting their final results. Louie and Charlie both ended up at WAAPA, Louie studying music and Charlie studying lighting and sound. When I moved out, at the start of this year, it was a tearful occasion.

'I'm going to miss you so much,' Aunty Jane whispered into my hair.

'Shush,' I said, willing myself not to cry.

'It's going to be so empty without you.'

'Stop it,' I said, 'we're still going to have coffee-and-paper every morning.'

'You promise?' she said.

'I promise.'

I got into the ute with Uncle Rob. We had the last of my things. I waved to her out of the window. 'See you tomorrow. I love you.'

'I love you too,' she said, waving madly. Within fifty metres Uncle Rob turned left onto the next street and pulled up outside an art deco unit.

'You sure this isn't too close?' he said. 'You know she'll be around here every five minutes.'

'It was the closest one I could find,' I said, lugging my suitcase up the stairs.

I pushed open the door to hear the music of my favourite musician, Nials Wisher, filling the front room.

'Hey,' he said, emerging from his studio, headphones around his neck, 'need a hand?'

I shook my head. 'Nah, all good.' I kissed Uncle Rob. 'See you tomorrow?'

'Tomorrow, kid,' he said as he left.

Frank and I made the decision to buy this two-storey unit when I finished studying. It hasn't been all smooth sailing — as I've learnt, life throws many challenges and tests along the way. But if you fail them, there's always a way to make amends. I was in third-year uni when Frank hit the big time. And I mean the screaming big time. He was picked up by a record label and played on commercial radio. He went from being an indie artist to an artist loved by the mainstream — he was playing gigs all over town and then he was scheduled for a world tour. I couldn't go — well, I could have, but that would have meant postponing my studies and living the life of a groupie. But it was Frank's dream, and as he had never held me back from anything I wanted to do, I wasn't going to hold him back either. I cut him loose, so he could live the life of a rock star and not have to feel obligated to some girl back home.

'You're not some girl,' Frank said, and I think it was the first time he was ever genuinely angry with me. 'What you're suggesting is that I'm going to go out, get pissed and have sex with groupies.'

I shook my head. 'I'm not suggesting that. I'm just making it so that if it happens, you don't have to feel like you've let me down.'

'What about you letting me down?' Frank said, 'by believing that is the kind of man I am?'

'I don't think that at all,' I said, 'I just know that long-distance relationships are hard. And your industry makes it even harder.'

'You can break up with me if you like,' Frank said, 'but for the record, I haven't broken up with you.'

When he left on his eight-month tour I was heartbroken. Chicco was not the same, not for me, not for the customers. Frank and I skyped a few times, but that was too painful so I'd cut the conversations short. I missed him too much and I didn't want him to feel trapped by me. I might sound like I was being really selfless, but again, it was my own fears and insecurities getting in the way. Underlying all of that behaviour was the self-doubt: why would Frank want me, when he could have anyone?

He returned a week early. He'd cancelled his final gig. I wasn't expecting him and it was almost closing time at Chicco. When he walked through the doors my heart actually leapt — I know it sounds corny, but if it's ever happened to you, you'll understand exactly that feeling. He held open his arms. 'Am I still welcome here, Shiraz?'

I snuggled into them. 'Of course you are,' I said, 'it's your father's shop.'

After that I decided that I didn't want to be apart from Frank for that long again. When he toured South-East Asia I went with him — who would turn down sandy beaches, perfect weather and lolling by a pool, when it was the middle of a miserable wet winter here? I found it was quite easy to study in five-star accommodation and so I kept on top of my uni work too. When we were in Indonesia, I hopped across to Bali, and to Kerobokan prison.

What a place! It's quite agricultural in many ways. I remember doing a tour of Fremantle Prison with school back in Year 8 and the tour guide telling us that because it had been built in the mid-1800s its facilities were outdated and its accommodation not fit for human habitation. It was all I thought about when entering Kerobokan: if only this place was half as nice as Freo. Jack had been on death row since his trial and guilty verdict, but just recently the president of Indonesia had commuted it to life imprisonment. I spoke to Maria before I left and she gave me a list of things (basic toiletries, clothes, shoes, cigarettes — anything worth trading in the system) to take to him. I was sitting on a bench waiting for him to arrive, looking at the bleakness and hostility of the environment and wondering how he was able to endure it.

The person walking towards me was nothing like the Jack I'd last seen crawling with scabies. This guy's posture and gait were more like the old Jack. As he neared I realised that, despite being in prison, he had put on weight. Gone was that emaciated and haggard face. When he smiled, however, I noticed his teeth hadn't fared well, but aside from that he was in pretty good condition.

'Hey Jazz,' he opened his arms, 'thanks for coming.'

'Jack,' I said. Hugging him back, I felt his taut body. He was thin, but he felt strong. 'You look good.'

'I know,' and then he laughed and screwed up his eyes like he used to. I nearly cried. 'Ironic, isn't it. I've been on death row for the last five years, yet it's actually saved my life.'

'It's incredible,' I said. Maria had told me of Jack's turnaround. Even in the early days, when death by execution squad hung over him daily, he had started to recover.

'I realised there was every chance I was going to die,' Jack said, 'and that was my epiphany. I didn't want to die — despite the fact I'd been doing everything in my power to fast-track myself there. And if I was going to die, I wasn't going to be a junkie. It was hard,' he shrugged, 'but really, what worth having in this life isn't hard?'

At that point another prisoner walked by and

shouted something to Jack in Indonesian. 'Excuse me,' he said, and turned to the prisoner, speaking in fast Indonesian. The other man commented and waved, then moved off.

'You speak Indonesian?' I said, amazed.

'Had to,' Jack said. 'Once I got here I realised I was the minority. If I didn't learn to speak their language I wasn't going to survive. In fact, that's what I do here. I teach English. It's partly what helped get my death sentence commuted. I also have a mentoring role, to the younger lads who are here for drug offences. It's a real passion of mine. And it feels good, you know. To actually contribute to bettering someone's life.'

When I left the prison I promised I'd return. And this time both he and I knew I meant it.

These days Frank and I schedule a stop in Bali on the way home to Perth whenever we've been overseas. It's not hard to fit in at least two visits a year with Jack. Frank sometimes goes out to Kerobokan on his own — he and Jack have their own friendship now. And I guess Frank was right, the friendship between Jack and me never ended. It suffered and it changed, but there is no doubt it still remains.

As for Tommy, I never saw him again after that day at the dealership — we move in totally different circles, so I have no idea if his life continued on its upward trajectory. But I can tell you now I hope it did. Reading back on the hatred I felt for Tommy makes me feel so sad for that young Jazz. Hating Tommy was like drinking poison — it only hurt me. Letting go (as Casey once said) was the only healthy thing to do. And as for Casey, we remain in contact via email. She's turned her jetsetting life into a permanent lifestyle. I never know where in the world she might be, until I receive a message from Kabul, or Goa, or Egypt. And whenever she's in town, we catch up. She is the only source of information I have on Annie.

It would be nice to say Annie eventually made a complete recovery, but she didn't. She improved a lot, but still remains in her parents' care and always will, unable to look after herself. I don't allow this information to make me hate myself anymore. I've done enough of that to last me a lifetime.

I accept Greenheadgate and the consequences of that night. All the wishing in the world never

changed a thing and all the hating in the world
fuelled the memories and kept it a strong force
in my life. I talk about that night sometimes with
people — students, patients — as an illustration of
how one event, no matter how catastrophic, takes
on a different meaning over time. I think the cliché
'time heals all wounds' is untrue. It doesn't heal
them as such, but it does allow for growth and
reflection. It changes them into something that can
be made more positive.

And as for Jasmine Lovely, the rapist, I now want to
state for the record I don't see myself by that label
anymore. Nothing will ever change the events of
that night, nothing will ever undo the damage and
nothing will ever make me stop feeling remorse for
everything that happened to everyone as a result.
But that Jasmine was a phantom I created, and the
real me survives today. I am able now to forgive
myself for that one stupid drunken night. I now
accept that I made a terrible mistake, one I thought
I'd never recover from, a mistake I truly believed
would plague me for the rest of my life. But I'm
happy to say that nothing is unsalvageable, that with

time things do improve and sometimes your biggest weaknesses can become your greatest strengths.

This closes Greenheadgate. A night that had ramifications beyond expectation, but also a night that opened the way for new experiences and relationships — for what are we if not the sum total of all we experience?

And so on that note, this time, dear reader, I finally, actually, really and truly, sign off.

The end

'

Need help?

If you are being bullied and/or sexually harassed there are many people who may be able to help, including parents, friends, older siblings, teachers and counsellors.

Some helpful websites:
- www.kidshelpline.com.au
- www.bullyingnoway.gov.au
- au.reachout.com
- www.esafety.gov.au
- www.eheadspace.org.au
- www.lifeline.org.au
- www.youthbeyondblue.com

Social media platforms have safety resources that you can use to report online bullying, such as:
- Facebook www.facebook.com/safety
- Instagram help.instagram.com/safety
- Snapchat www.snapchat.com/safety

Acknowledgements

I have to thank my students at Sacred Heart College who 'willingly' participated in early readings of the manuscript and gently guided me through the use of technology and current language. In particular, my Year 10 Academic Extension class — who made it part of their year's work to read and review draft copies — Tess, Eva, Olivia, Kate, Bianca, Dillon, Medbh, Nadya, Meg, Miranda, Alyssa, Steph, Dylan, Matt and Elijah, and also thank you to my colleagues in the English Department for your time and feedback.

To my sister and my mum, thank you for your raw and honest feedback; Jane — I'm sorry this didn't come with an emotional warning and Mum, yes, sadly, this is a world you don't know. Thanks always to Savannah and Willow for helping me navigate Snapchat and Instagram and ignoring the unwashed clothes building in the laundry and 'fend for yourself' dinners. Thank you Nick for being my constant supporter, for your feedback, love and continual encouragement.

To Cate Sutherland, as always, I'm grateful for your vision when I pass over the rather dodgy manuscript — you always possess the ability to see what it might become. Naama, your precision and diligence is certainly what whipped this manuscript into shape, it has been an absolute pleasure working with you on this. To all at Fremantle Press, thank you.

While all my work is fiction, the events I write of are shaped by happenings to real people. The worlds of my stories are familiar to many, and totally alien to others. And so, dear reader, I thank you. I appreciate the opportunity to explore them with you.

Kate McCaffrey, 2016.

Kate McCaffrey

Kate grew up in Perth's northern suburbs. She has a degree in English and Art and a diploma in Education.

Kate is the author of award-winning novels for young adults: *Destroying Avalon* (2006), winner of the WAYRBA Avis Page Award for older readers and the Western Australian Premier's Book Award for Young Adults; *In Ecstasy* (2008), winner of the Australian Family Therapists' Award for Children's Literature; *Beautiful Monster* (2010), named a 2011 White Raven, selected from newly published books from around the world as especially noteworthy by the International Youth Library in Munich, Germany; and *Crashing Down* (2014), winner of the Australian Family Therapists' Award for Children's Literature.

Find out more about Kate and her work at katemccaffrey.wordpress.com

KATE
McCAFFREY
Best-selling author of Saving Jazz

DESTROYING
Avalon

KATE
McCAFFREY
Best-selling author of Destroying Avalon

CRASHING
down

KATE
McCAFFREY
Best-selling author of Saving Jazz

BEAUTIFUL
Monster

KATE
McCAFFREY
Best-selling author of Destroying Avalon

In Ecstasy

First published 2016 by
FREMANTLE PRESS

Fremantle Press Inc. trading as Fremantle Press
PO Box 158, North Fremantle, Western Australia, 6159
fremantlepress.com.au

Copyright © Kate McCaffrey, 2016.

The moral rights of the author have been asserted.

Cover photograph: janifest/Adobe Stock.

 A catalogue record for this
book is available from the
National Library of Australia

ISBN 9781925163582 (paperback)
ISBN 9781925163605 (ebook)

Fremantle Press is supported by the Western Australian State
Government through the Department of Cultural Industries,
Tourism and Sport.

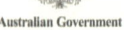 

Publication of this title was assisted by the Commonwealth
Government through Creative Australia, its arts funding and
advisory body.

Fremantle Press respectfully acknowledges the Whadjuk people
of the Noongar nation as the Traditional Owners and Custodians
of the land where we work in Walyalup.